CRITICAL ACCLAIM FOR *ROULETTE*

"In their atmospheric new mystery-thriller *Roulette*, Locke and Guptara grab the reader's attention instantly with an appalling scenario in bucolic north Florida. The authors place their sympathetic crime-fighters in a deceptively benign rural atmosphere where, nonetheless, time is running out and death and destruction beckon."
—Patrick H. Moore, author of *27 Days* and *Setting the Record Straight*

"*Roulette* sets a new bar for intrigue. I could not set this book down. Bottom line: *Roulette* is for you if you love conspiracy thrillers moving with the speed of an air boat and a mind-blowing, animalistic bite."
—TG Wolff, author and co-creator of *Mysteries to Die For Podcast*

"Great writing!"
—Andrew F. Gulli, Managing Editor, *The Strand Magazine*

ROULETTE

BOOKS BY THOMAS LOCKE AND JYOTI GUPTARA

Fortune's Favor
Roulette

ALSO BY THOMAS LOCKE

Emissary
Merchant of Alyss
Recruits, Renegades
Trial Run
Flash Point
Fault Lines

ALSO BY JYOTI GUPTARA

Conspiracy of Calaspia
Calaspia. Der Schwertkodex
Calaspia. Das Erbe der Apheristen
The Conversation Doctor
The Promise of the Sky
Business Storytelling from Hype to Hack

THOMAS LOCKE
JYOTI GUPTARA

ROULETTE
A THRILLER

Copyright © 2023 by Thomas Locke and Jyoti Guptara

All rights reserved. No part of the book may be reproduced in any form or by any electronic or mechanical means, including information storage and retrieval systems, without permission in writing from the publisher, except by a reviewer who may quote brief passages in a review.

Down & Out Books
3959 Van Dyke Road, Suite 265
Lutz, FL 33558
DownAndOutBooks.com

The characters and events in this book are fictitious. Any similarity to real persons, living or dead, is coincidental and not intended by the author.

Cover design by Miley Miller

ISBN: 1-64396-342-2
ISBN-13: 978-1-64396-342-6

*For the boys
And 'Dr. Stu', mad scientist
Thank you for not becoming an evil genius*

Carol Steen slipped behind the ER main desk just as the phone started ringing. She waved a farewell to the departing duty nurse, then spoke the words for the first time that shift. "Urgent Care."

Her husband, the sheriff of Alachua County, asked, "That you, Carol?"

"Sorry, that particular lady has left for the Bahamas."

Dewey Steen showed the world a stern lawman's face, but underneath he possessed a secret streak of courtly good manners. "I been meaning to ask when we were taking off on that long weekend."

"There is the small matter," Carol said, "of our jobs."

"Oh. Them."

"What can I do for you, hon?"

It was easy to be blinded by the man's ruddy good looks and good-old-boy grin and miss the fact that an extremely able county sheriff occupied the space behind those glittering grey eyes. "We caught wind of a rave."

"Where?"

"Out Route 60. Probably in one of those empty warehouses."

Route 60 placed it in county's bailiwick. Inside the Gainesville city limits, all emergency cases were shipped to the University of

Florida's medical center, which was five times the size of the county hospital. "We're a little short-staffed, Dewey."

"I'm calling the university hospital next. May be nothing. But I just wanted to give you a heads-up."

"I'll alert the team."

"That's my lady. If I get a minute, I'll stop by for a howdy."

The survey of her little medical empire took all of two minutes, as Carol knew it would. The extremely capable day-shift nurse would have ensured that every station was spotless and fully stocked before closing out her files.

There was a possible cardiac arrest in three. Two more patients were waiting transport, one to radiology and the other to a bed on the non-critical third floor. Their new resident doctor was in with the heart. Otherwise things were calm. But it being a Thursday night, that would soon change. This close to the summer recess, weekends tended to expand.

Carol was back behind the admissions desk when Dr. Henry entered and said, "Good evening, Carol."

"Doctor."

The hospital's chief internist possessed an unflappable dignity, a solemn calm that reassured the most terrified patient. His name was Henri Beausejour, and he was from the Dominican Republic. When he had grown tired of staff butchering his last name, he suggested they call him Dr. Henri. But the correct French pronunciation was too much for the locals, and within a month he had become Dr. Henry. And Dr. Henry he remained. "We'll be gathering in the staff room in five minutes."

"I'll be ready."

The Alachua County Medical Center had been built with University of Florida money. There were a number of such projects dotted around the region, attempts to keep the local populace on the university's side. UF employed more than half the county's workforce. During term time, the county's population tripled. There were enormous problems associated with the university's dominant presence. More than half the student population came from out of state. This did not sit well with many of the locals. Central Florida remained staunchly conservative, its mentality and way of life more in keeping with southern Georgia. Building a new county hospital did not stop the resentment, but it did dampen the outrage.

The ER nurses station was shaped like a quarter-moon and faced the main entrance. The waiting area was sectioned off, a big room to her right with a glass wall so Carol's team could observe everything going on inside. The curved desk where she sat was high-tech central. Big-screen monitors showed pictures of all the rooms. Cameras were focused on the faces in the beds. Beside these pictures were the rolling vitals for each patient, heart rate and respiration and blood pressure. Below these were the room number and patient's name and ID.

The first two hours of her shift were quiet, almost tomb-like. The clock on the wall above the main entrance seemed frozen. Then they had five criticals come in almost simultaneously, boom-boom-boom. A heart attack, a stroke, and three victims of a two-car collision. This filled up the closest rooms and got things moving. Dr. Henry handled them well enough. He was in fact an excellent doctor. But Carol disliked how he tended to linger, even when they faced multiple incoming patients. That was the problem with sharing their chief doctor with another ward, instead of having an ER specialist in charge of the shift. An emergency room doctor was supposed to stabilize the patient, deal with life-threatening issues, order any necessary tests, then move on. Dr. Henry wanted to remain and supervise the patient and enter into the healing process. It was his nature as a trained internist. But ER work was not about healing. It was about ensuring every patient's survival.

Which meant that in a crush Carol had to rely heavily on the resident.

And this was where the problems started.

The medical resident on night duty was named Stacie Swann. She was an attractive dark-haired woman in her early thirties and hailed from Richmond by way of the UF medical school. Why the resident doctor had ever entered ER care, Carol had no idea. A good ER doctor maintained a singular calm. Even when blood spattered the wall and everyone was screaming, the doctor had to remain detached, focused, in control. When multiple emergencies struck, the ER doctor was the rock everyone clung to, staff and patients alike. Stacie Swann possessed too much of a sultry spark. She took time between patients to check her hair and her appearance. She was too aware of herself, the sort of attractive woman who liked to pretend she was the center of the universe. Carol was waiting for the crisis when everything hidden inside that woman exploded in all their faces.

Just after one in the morning, Carol was drawn from the accident patients by the sound of their red phone. The phone was actually not colored any differently from the others. It was simply their name for the crisis phone. The Gainesville police had that number, and the ambulance operators, the sheriff's office, the staties, the local doctors, a few others, not many. The phone did not ring. It chirped. After a very bad shift, Carol sometimes dreamed that she heard that chirp, at home where she was supposed to be safe and protected. She always woke up screaming.

The county's chief ambulance driver was a tall rawboned man named Previtt. He took a Florida cracker's pride in only going by one name. Previtt was very handsome, in a woodsy and angular fashion. When he became agitated his hands and body were never still, shifting, adjusting his clothes, clearing his throat. It made some people very nervous to be around him. But Carol knew Previtt to be solid, no matter what the crisis. His nervous twitches didn't bother her at all. Unlike Stacie Swann, who found it a trial to be in the same room with Previtt. If Carol had not already liked the lanky Previtt before, that would have done it for her.

Previtt said, "Incoming with three ravers. Two comatose, one jumping out of her skin."

"Any idea what they're on?"

"I keep asking but they ain't saying." In the background was a high keening sound, like a human band saw, overwhelming even the siren. Previtt's voice remained as untouched as usual. "We're fifteen minutes out."

Carol alerted her staff, then swiftly saw to the two patients in the waiting room. A young pregnant woman with stomach pains, probably gas. She checked the woman's vitals, looked for bleeding, gave her an over-the-counter antacid, and moved on to a young Latina with an ulcerated eye. This second woman should have been checked by a doctor days before. But it did no good to scold. The county hospital saw an increasing number of undocumented guest workers. Nowadays the center only hired ER staff with a working knowledge of Spanish. Patients like this woman usually came in late at night so as to receive help with the minimum of questions. Carol hurried the patient into an empty room and asked Stacie Swann to come have a look.

The resident continued to adjust the stroke victim's IV. "I'm busy."

Carol could see the patient was stable. "We have three inbound and—"

"In a minute."

"Thank you, Doctor." It was a typical exchange. Carol walked back down the hall and coded the electronic lock for the ER pharmacy. The room cameras would show Carol had spoken with the doctor. The rooms were not wired for sound. If anyone asked, it would be Carol's word against the doctor's recollection. But no one would ask.

Carol took the eye salve and drops and signed the drug sheet, placing in the line by her name, 'under the advisement of Dr. Swann.' She treated the patient's eye, taped a gauze bandage into place, and explained that the woman was to apply the salve three times daily until it ran out, then she could uncover it and begin using the drops.

Carol went back to check on the pregnant woman with stomach pains, but the patient had departed. The waiting room was empty save for the Latina's husband and three sleeping children. This was also typical, how the undocumented workers seldom arrived alone. When the patient rejoined her family, they all thanked Carol with an almost musical desperation.

A distant siren alerted Carol to an incoming ambulance. She bundled the family toward the exit, then hurried to alert the staff. But just as she started down the main corridor, the woman called, "Signora, please excuse me. You must come!"

Carol turned back, ready to snap, when she realized the Latina stood there alone, framed by the yellow overheads of the ER's covered entrance. The children stood in the circular drive, wailing. Carol's first thought was, the husband had suffered a heart attack on their doorstep.

Then she stepped through the entrance and saw the girl.

Even in her extremely disheveled state, she remained a very pretty young woman. Vomit stained the front of her sparkly dress. The short dark skirt was hiked up to reveal muscular legs. Her feet were bare, the toes curled so tight she appeared to be trying to make fists with her feet. The young woman was aged somewhere around twenty, her grey eyes so dilated they looked almost black. Her back was arched at an impossible angle, her fingers clawing the concrete sidewalk.

She had been dumped.

They saw an increasing number of such cases. A group of kids partied in someone's house. One of them became so ill their situation broke through the others' drug fog. They were terrified of revealing themselves. Calling 911 meant police and questions and a record. So they drove the victim over, waited for a quiet moment, then dumped them by the ER entrance.

Carol turned and yelled through the open doorway, "*Code red! Code red!*"

A nurse and male orderly rushed out just as the ambulance pulled under the arch. The Latina family had vanished. Previtt leapt from the ambo and helped them stabilize the woman into a neck brace, then lifted her up far enough for Carol to check the spine. "All right, let's shift her."

Together they lifted her onto the gurney and pulled her inside. Dr. Henry and the other staff nurse were outside, pulling the screamer from the ambo. Dr. Swann and the orderly were inside the ambo, checking the vital signs of the two quiet vics. Previtt and the orderly helped shift the dumped patient onto a bed. Carol fastened the restraining braces around the patient's ankles and wrists to keep her from rolling out of the gurney or clawing the IV needles from her arm.

Previtt said, "I got a call five minutes out. Four more vics waiting at the rave."

"Tell one of the nurses to alert Shands," Carol said, naming the university medical center. "And check the sidewalk on your way out, see if there's a purse or wallet. We need to ID her."

"You got it." He was gone.

"My name is Carol Steen. I am a nurse at County Hospital. Can you hear me? What's your name?" She spoke at one notch below a full shout. She did not expect the woman to respond. It was amazing how often the patients would tell her, hours or days later, that just hearing Carol tell them they had arrived at the hospital drew them back from the brink. "You're safe now. We're going to try and stabilize you. But it would help if you told us—"

Stacie Swann hurried up beside her. "What do we have?"

Carol replied, "My guess is, another PDP."

Prescription drug parties had only recently arrived in their region. According to police investigations, PDPs had been imported from up north by students at the University of Florida. Now they were a growing rage. Young people filled a candy dish with an assortment of prescription medicines taken from various family members or bought on the street. They went around in a circle, popping whatever they picked up, usually downing the tablets with alcohol.

Stacie asked, "Was there any ID?"

"Not that we've found. There usually isn't one when they're dumped."

Stacie Swann leaned in close to the woman and shouted, "Can you hear me? What is your name?"

The woman's eyes were rolled back so far only the whites showed. She was arched to the point that the foam in the neck brace crackled and pinched.

The doctor asked, "Vitals?"

"Heart rate 147. Blood pressure off the map, two hundred over a hundred—"

The patient chose that moment to go into another spasm. Carol and the doctor fought to hold the woman down. A trace of the doctor's perfume drifted in the air. If Stacie Swann had been a nurse, Carol would have ordered her to wash it off and in the future use nothing with a lingering odor. The power of smell was vital to saving lives in this place. But Stacie Swann was a doctor, so Carol had not ever spoken about it. Even so, it irritated her, drawing her away from the work at hand. She made a mental note to speak with Dr. Henry.

Carol was positioned up closer to the patient's head, so she was the one who heard the soft keening noises, a tight *hee-hee-hee* with each rapid indrawn breath. She freed one hand by leaning her body against the fouled front of the party dress and undid the Velcro strap holding the neck brace in place. She felt the woman's throat. There was something wrong.

The resident doctor cried, "Fifty cc's of Adaman!"

Adaman was a standard treatment for extreme agitation, along with Valium. But Carol remained where she was. "Doctor, you need to address the airway."

"You heard me! Do it *now!*"

Carol had retreated to that detached calm that served her well through any number of multiple crises. She could hear the doctor's frantic breathing, almost in time with the victim's. *Stacie Swann has never seen a patient flip out before*, Carol realized. She heard the metallic flatness to her own voice as she said, "Her air passage is blocked, Doctor."

"Look! *I'm* the doctor here!"

Carol got in close enough to show the rage beneath the calm. "Then stop acting like my teenage daughter in a tantrum and *behave* like one."

Even with the patient heaving against them and her straps, the doctor was shocked from her panic. "What?"

"Remember your ABCs." It was the first lesson drilled into every ER doctor and nurse. The first three vitals to be checked on every incoming patient. Airway, breathing, circulation. "You've got to stop her bucking. The muscles of her neck are constricted. She can't get air into her lungs."

The doctor shifted around so she could see over Carol's body. "We need..."

"That's right, doctor. We need to paralyze her before we introduce a calming agent. Why don't you set it up? I can hold her."

The doctor kept glancing Carol's way as she coded the lock on the emergency drug kit and took out the syringe loaded with Pancuronium. Swann fitted it into the IV and pushed the plunger. "I should have thought of that."

It was as close to an apology as Carol had ever received from a doctor in a crisis. "Thank you, Doctor."

Stacie Swann shifted her attention to the monitors. "Heart and blood pressure are dropping."

Carol released her hold and stepped back. "The patient's breathing has eased."

Stacie fitted the stethoscope into her ears. "What do you think she's on?"

"Who knows? A cocktail, more than likely. They're mixing ecstasy with just about everything these days. Dewey's been hearing things."

Swann slipped the stethoscope back into her pocket. "What does the sheriff say?"

"Some new dealer is trying to break into the local university market. The state labs fear they're putting together a witches' brew of heroin and meth and Valium. The symptoms are unlike..." But Carol was hardly paying attention to her own words.

"Something's wrong."

"I...What?"

"The patient is not stabilizing." She sensed it before the monitors registered the change. "Heart rate is still dropping."

"Blood pressure is tanking!" The panic returned to the resident's voice. "Did I get the dose wrong?"

Carol checked the syringe's packaging. "Fifteen mils, the prescribed amount."

"Maybe it's an allergic reaction?"

"No known allergies to Pancuronium. Not even when the victim has taken a drug cocktail." Carol felt the fingers. The hands had grown icy cold. "Circulation is almost nil."

"Lift her head." Stacie Swann began running her hands through the victim's hair. "No sign of injuries to skull. Subdural hematoma unlikely."

Carol checked the legs. "No visible bruising to limbs."

"Blood pressure down to sixty-five over thirty and still falling!" The monitor emitted a whining alarm which magnified the confused fear in Stacie's voice. But now there was a difference to the resident. She might be toying with full-blown panic, but her hands and brain remained very busy, very connected. "Pelvis is stable. Belly not rigid."

"No visible swelling to joints."

"Let's roll her over."

Carol unlatched the braces. There was no longer any need for restraints. "I checked the spine before we put her on the gurney. She appeared to be..."

Then the patient woke up.

The standard return to wakefulness from a near-coma state was gradual. There was a measured increase in heart rate and respiration. The patient normally moaned, there was often some thrashing about, the result of random impulses sent by a brain returning from the brink.

This time was different.

The monitor's alarm went silent. The heart-rate beep

accelerated. Not gradually. It simply went from near-coma to full adrenaline flight. Carol was not certain of the rate. She could not spare a glance at the monitor.

Because the patient chose that moment to open her eyes.

The pupils were still somewhat dilated. But the standard round shape was gone. Instead, they seemed to have become elongated. Like a feral beast had suddenly crawled out of its lair and was watching Carol.

The victim's features drew back so taut blood could not push through to the upper layers of skin. Carol's own heart rate might have accelerated to match the pinging monitor, but her vision was crystal clear and her mind remained held by the ER detachment. She saw how the cheeks became white as bone, how the mouth drew back from the teeth, how the eyes were now narrow slits and the ears seemed clenched to the sides of her skull.

Then the woman snarled.

The sound was so vicious both Stacie and Carol lurched back from the bed. For the first time in a very long while, Carol was actually afraid for her life.

The victim arched her back, her slitted gaze still watching them. Still snarling. Guttural sounds that punched up from the writhing stomach. The writhing was not a spasm. Instead, Carol had the impression of watching a lioness rise from slumber.

The young woman leapt from the bed. It was a bounding motion, that of a feral beast suddenly discovering it was no longer chained.

She tore through the door. Carol scrambled over to watch the victim sprint down the hall. Bounding on all fours. Not running. *Loping.*

Someone in the hall screamed. But the patient had already raced past.

As their patient leapt through the entrance, she howled. Like a wolf.

Then she vanished into the night.

The Gainesville townhouse was both functional and cheery, freshly painted and furnished with a professional decorator's eye for detail. There was even a silver-framed photograph on the kitchen counter of a beautiful young woman, smiling for the camera and holding a bundle of daffodils. The realtor who showed Eric around explained that the townhouse served as the builder's demo unit. But this was April, and the local real estate market would remain fairly dormant until school restarted in September. So the builder was happy to rent it on a short-term basis. So long as the builder could show it to possible buyers. Which required a professional cleaner to come in every other day, and the cost was included with all the other fees.

Eric already had his checkbook out. "First and last month's rent and a deposit okay? I want to move in this afternoon."

The realtor used her cellphone to check his references while Eric unloaded the rear of his SUV. When the realtor left, Eric retraced his steps to a Publix supermarket he had spotted on the way over. He went back and made himself a meal of cheese and cold-cuts and salad, then set the alarm on his wristwatch and lay down.

When his watch chimed the hour before sunset, Eric was already up and stretching. He took his time, working out the kinks from eleven hours on the road. At a quarter to six, he set the house alarm and let himself out the rear door. The sun was a blistering globe a few degrees above the western horizon. Eric shouldered his pack, adjusted the drinking tube, and slipped through the rear gate. There were a number of other late-afternoon joggers, a few cyclists, two couples, and a father pushing a pram with what appeared to be twins. Eric followed the trail east, paralleling University Avenue. His destination was the Morningside Nature Center, a beautiful enclave that lay between the Gainesville Airport and Newnans Lake.

He found the rest area was just where he had been told, a small park at the top of what passed for a hill in Florida. Through the surrounding pines, the lake's surface glistened a ruddy gold in the fading daylight. Eric used a picnic table to stretch while he waited for his contact.

The sheriff's car rolled through the pine-covered gravel twenty minutes late. Twenty minutes for a local cop on county-wide patrol was nothing. Eric rose from the table where he had been pretending to admire the sunset. The sheriff's window rolled down to reveal a stern expression and focused cop eyes. "You Bannon?"

"Yes."

"Let's see some ID."

Eric pulled his license from the pack. Sheriff Dewey Steen took his time over it, typing the name into his computer. "Hop on in."

As the car rolled out of the park area, Steen said, "I spent four months trying to get the DEA folks to wake up and pay attention. Finally gave up. Seemed like they wanted me to go out there and solve the problem, arrest the perps, and invite them in to take the credit. Then out of nowhere I get a call asking me to extend to you every courtesy. What I want to know is, are you here to help or to give me another headache I don't need?"

"Probably a little of both," Eric replied.

Dewey gave him a cop's smile, a new glimmer to the eyes and very little else. "So what are you, some kind of secret agent?"

"I'm a forensic accountant."

Dewey Steen had hands the size of mitts and arms to match, big tough branches sprouting from a solid trunk of a frame. He dominated the front seat, a palpable force, easily capable of subduing anything thrown his way. "You want my help, you're gonna have to unlock that door."

"I used to be with the State Department's intelligence arm. I left them seven years ago. Now I'm freelance."

"Who do you answer to?" When Eric hesitated, Steen pushed. "Trust works both ways or it don't work at all."

"This time, I'm answering directly to the White House."

Steen said, "So, this ain't just about some local drug problem we're having."

"We're investigating a much larger issue. We think they're connected to what you've been seeing."

"Will you tell me what that issue is?"

Eric took his time responding. "Maybe. If you're sure you want to know. And if it's relevant to your investigation. Yes. I'll tell you."

Eric had studied the region enough to be able to follow the sheriff's journey. The cruiser turned onto East University Drive and followed it around the southern edge of the nature center to where it joined with NE 55th. This became Highway 26 as it fronted the northeast shore of Newnans Lake. Dewey Steen drove around Gainesville's regional airport and entered an industrial zone made up of low-rent warehouses.

When Sheriff Dewey Steen cut off the engine, Eric heard the lowing of cattle through his open window. Highway traffic rumbled in the distance. Dewey gave Eric time to inspect the rubble-filled parking area, then asked, "Know what you're looking at?"

"A rave site." There was no mistaking the scene. Ahead of them, the warehouse bay doors were wide open. The remnants of a stage could be seen at the depot's far end. The litter was knee deep in places, bottles and bonfire ashes and beer cans and clothing. "Why are we here?"

"Got someone I want you to meet." Dewey Steen slipped his

cellphone from his pocket and punched in a number. "Where are you, Tyler?"

In reply, a car rumbled throatily as it emerged from between two distant buildings. Eric rose from the sheriff's car as the Dodge Charger rolled up and stopped. A young man slipped from behind the wheel and called over, "Who's this, Uncle Dewey?"

"Get your sorry hide on over here."

Glass crunched underfoot as the young man walked over. "He a cop?"

"That don't matter none. It's me you got to worry about."

He was a good-looking kid, even when frightened. The setting sun revealed a very fit young man of perhaps twenty, with blond hair and chiseled features and the solid bulk of a football player in his prime.

"Tyler here got caught up in the sweep when we shut this place down. His scholarship is hanging by a thread. Ain't that right?"

"You got me here," the young man said sullenly. "Now what?"

"Stow that lip in your back pocket and tell the man what you told my deputy."

Tyler kicked at the refuse by his feet. A broken syringe bounced over to rest by Eric's foot. "I ain't never seen a cop dressed for a jog before."

"Tyler, I'm not asking you again."

"They showed up like usual."

"Which I take to mean this wasn't your first rave." Dewey Steen shook his head like an angry bull. "I got a mind—"

Eric halted the sheriff with a hand to his shoulder. "Who is 'they,' Tyler?"

"You know. The players."

"The people dealing in the drugs."

"No, man. You got drugs everywhere. All the time. Long before the rave gets going."

"All right. So you're telling me these so-called players are special."

Dewey groused, "I can't believe I'm hearing my sister's boy talk like he's an insider."

"Tyler is doing exactly what you told him to do," Eric replied. When the sheriff did not respond, Eric said to the young man, "I'm not interested in messing up your life. But I need you to help me understand."

Dewey Steen muttered, "Tyler's done a fine job of messing things up his own self."

"Dewey." Eric waited until he was certain the sheriff was going to stay quiet, then said, "Tell me about the players."

The kid's eyes glittered fearfully as the perimeter lights clicked on. "That's what they're called. I ain't never seen one up close."

"But you know when they show up."

"Everybody does. The place just amps up a notch, like the starting gun's just gone off."

"What are they dealing?" When the kid hesitated, Eric said, "Help me out, Tyler. I'm trying to get a handle on a new situation before it blows up in our faces."

"The stuff is called roulette."

Eric glanced at the sheriff, who frowned and shook his head. "How long has it been around?"

"I dunno. I only been to a couple of these things. Honest, Uncle Dewey. But it seems like everybody's talking about this stuff."

"Where do you go to school?"

"UF. That's where I heard about last night's rave."

"Has roulette been around for a while?"

"Naw, man, I'm telling you, this stuff is totally new."

"So when did you first hear about it?"

"Been three, maybe four months now. We got invited to play in the Sugar Bowl. When things slowed down after, I find out everybody is whispering about this new high."

Eric turned to Dewey and said, "Sheriff, why don't you take a look around the place, see if there's anything that might help us out."

Glass scrunched beneath the sheriff's boots as he stomped off, kicking refuse and muttering to himself. Eric probed gently, "Do you snort roulette?"

"No way, man. You get a skin patch. You put this stuff up your nose, I expect you'd be looking down at the dark side of the moon."

"It's powerful, then."

"Oh, yeah." He shrugged. "But it depends."

"On what?"

The kid's words jerked slightly with the adrenaline rush and the fear. "Every time is different. That's why it's called roulette. One time it's a mild sort of glow, just keeps you mellow and happy all night long. The next, and man, you ain't *never* been where this takes you."

"Do you hallucinate?"

"I only took it a few times. I ain't never seen nothing, you know, like the walls melting and stuff. But yeah, you trip. Sort of." The football player was bopping now, coming up on the balls of his feet, jerking like he was ready to burst out onto the field. "Mostly I just feel invincible. Like I could take on the whole opposing team, carry them right down to the end zone all by my lonesome. Easy as you please."

"Ecstasy is often mixed with meth or another speed. The effect is like you're describing. Bursts of energy that can last for hours."

"Naw, this ain't nothing like what you're saying." He glanced over to make sure his uncle was out of hearing range, then said, "This stuff makes you feel like king of the world. Like everything you had in you was just amped up a hundred times. Whatever you are, it just gets way bigger."

Eric nodded like he understood. He turned and called, "Sheriff." When Dewey rejoined them, Eric said to the kid, "You think you could tell me when you hear of the next rave?"

"Oh, man, I don't know…"

Dewey did not need volume to add menace to his words. "You can help us out or you can spend your summer inside my holding pen, watching the shadows crawl. See your scholarship vanish, lose any hope you might have of going pro, finish your days up at some community college. It's your choice, Tyler."

"Yeah, sure. I guess. But you got to promise nobody will ever know, I mean…"

"Your name won't appear anywhere. Isn't that right, Sheriff?"

"Naw, it ain't that. These players, they don't mess around. I heard some things, man, these are some tough cats. Especially this dude called Ryker."

Eric closed the distance between him and the kid. Close enough to see that Tyler was terrified. "Tell us what you know."

"They're animals, him and his crew. Beasts of the night."

"What's that supposed to mean?"

Dewey scoffed, "Legends. They'll tell the kids anything to protect their secrecy."

"Meant to frighten you," Eric said. "Meant to warn you off."

"No, man. You get on the bad side of these players, they'll tear you apart. Only reason people mess with them players at all is, you can't find roulette except through them." Tyler was already backing away. "You just keep my name out of it, you hear?"

Eric had Dewey drop him off along the running trail, well removed from his townhouse. He jogged back, let himself into the house, took his time stretching and showering, then placed the call.

His contact answered with, "Is this line secure?"

"Roger that."

The scrambler gave the man's voice a slightly metallic edge. "You weren't supposed to make contact until you had something to report."

"Which is why I'm calling."

"You already have confirmation?"

"Yes."

"Are you certain?"

"One eyewitness. But the evidence is clear."

The line hissed slightly. Eric stepped over to where he could study the last glimmer of daylight. Eric's contact was known for instantaneous decisions. He demanded rapid-fire reports, distilled down to bullets of intel. To have the Washington power guy ponder like this reflected the situation's magnitude.

Finally his boss asked, "When do you expect further confirmation?"

"I'm due to make the rounds with the local sheriff in ninety minutes."

The sigh carried an electric hiss. "So it's as bad as we feared."

"Oh, no," Eric replied. "It's much worse than that."

The rest of the shift ran smoothly enough for Carol to stow away the early scare. This was a vital part of ER work, being able to compartmentalize. Carol drove home, slept well, rose in the late morning, and started her normal Friday routine. She did not forget things like a woman loping on all fours down the ER's hall. Instead, by the time she left for her Friday evening shift, she had put it down to another young person riding off to the OD Corral.

Handling the crazies of this world was part of her job description.

The chief day nurse was an unflappable African American named Harriett. The day's files were perfect as usual, the station impeccable. Harriett had enough seniority to reserve her weekends for her grandchildren. She lingered a bit as Carol settled in. "Understand you had some fireworks last night."

"What did you hear?"

"Pretty young thing got dumped. She woke up and did a runner on you."

"For once, the rumors are correct."

"Used to be, by late spring the county outside Gainesville gradually turned back to the way I knew as a kid." Harriett bundled up her sweater and purse and keys and insulated mug. "Guess the place had to grow up someday. You have yourself a quiet night."

Carol watched the doors slide shut and stared at her reflection in the glass. Her mind flashed back to the woman howling. Like a wolf.

Weekend nights went through distinct transitions. Before midnight, many patients were indigents. Illegal immigrants working the orange groves, or cleaning local businesses, or cutting the lawns of university professors, or tending the horses of breeders between Gainesville and Ocala. By ten thirty, their waiting room was packed, but silent. Even the children were well-behaved. These people were used to waiting.

Half an hour later, Carol was drawn from her routine by the sound of weeping.

Tears were not at all unusual in ER. What made the sound unique was that it came from their pharmacy.

Carol coded the lock. The door chimed as she entered, interrupting the doctor's crying jag. "Stacie?" As she bent over the young woman, Carol realized she had never used the resident doctor's first name before. "What's the matter?"

Stacie Swann wore a clown's mask. Mascara flowed all the way to her chin. "Men are such pigs."

The pharmacy had a pair of leather-topped stools on rollers that normally were tucked under the narrow ledge the nurses and pharmacist used as a desk. Carol pulled out the second but did not sit down. "Some are."

"All of them. Every last one. I should know. I've tested enough to have a clinical sample of the entire rotten masculine race."

"I'm going to leave you long enough to get a wet towel. We need to clean your face."

Stacie rubbed her cheek, spreading mascara across her nose. "I want a milkshake."

"That's an excellent idea. We'll go get one together. But first we have to make it through the rest of shift."

Carol slipped into the staff room, wet a clean towel, then picked up a second dry one. As she walked back around the nurse's station, Dr. Henry left a patient's cubicle. "Carol, what's going on in there?"

"Don't ask." She let herself back into the pharmacy and wiped the doctor's face as she would a child.

"I don't even know why I'm crying. We broke up over a year ago." Stacie's voice was melodious in sorrow, the Virginia lilt much stronger now. "I caught him cheating on me. Now Momma just called to say he's marrying my *cousin*."

"There. All better." Carol dropped the stained wet towel to the floor and patted her face with the dry one. Soft, comforting strokes. "I'm so sorry."

The doctor sniffed loudly and wiped her nose with the dry towel. "Are the patients backing up out there?"

"Nothing that can't wait a few more minutes."

"My cousin is such a tramp. Beautiful in a trashy sort of way." The doctor fought off a case of chin tremors. "I thought he was the one."

"Were you engaged?"

"Nothing official. We'd talked about it. No date." She blew her nose once more. "But that doesn't make it right."

"No, of course it doesn't."

"Name me one man who's not a total louse."

"Dwight Edward Steen."

"Who?"

"My husband of twenty-two years. I have put him through ten kinds of misery. When I try to apologize, Dewey says he's never loved me more. And I believe him."

Stacie looked at her. Carol watched the younger woman slowly draw the world back into focus. "I'd like to meet a good man."

"You will. Soon as shift ends, we'll get us milkshakes and swing by the house." Carol stood. "Ready?"

An hour later, Carol was on the desk when the call came in. For once, Previtt's cracker calm was shaken. "Ah, who's on duty over there?"

She flipped the microphone. "It's Carol. What's the matter?"

"I'm inbound. Got a, well, tell you the truth, I don't know what I've got."

"Hold one." Several fathers leaned on the glass wall separating the full waiting room from the entrance lobby. They were all watching her and listening. The radio system connecting the central station to the ambulance and police had a hook-up to a wireless earpiece. No one liked to use the Bluetooth earphone because it tended to fall off at the most inconvenient times, such as when the user was bending over a frantic patient. But on busy nights when no one could be spared to stay on full-time desk duty, the earpiece was essential. She slipped the plastic hook around her ear and flipped the switch to turn off the speaker. "All right, I'm here. What's going on?"

"We got called to an accident. Strictly as backup."

There had been a single-car accident on the Turnpike exit closest to Gainesville. Carol had heard the initial alert. The highway patrol reported no serious injury. But it was standard ops in a highway incident for an ambulance to be called in. "How many victims?"

"Right out of the accident, didn't appear to be any. But I was standing there, chewing the fat with the cops, and one guy went into spasms."

"You mean, a seizure?"

"I mean, I don't know."

"Previtt, why don't I hear the siren?"

"On account of how, we load the guy up and pull away, and he goes calm. More than that. He's back there snoring away."

"Is this some kind of joke?" The sharp tone to her voice caught Stacie Swann as she passed around the station, reaching for the next patient's file.

"Stan is sitting back there beside the vic." Stan was Previtt's number two. Carol could hear him speak. Previtt passed on, "The vic's vitals are stable. The guy is just zonked. You want me to hold the mike back where you can hear him snore?"

Stacie asked, "What's wrong?"

"Hold one, Previtt." Carol made a fist around the mike and told the resident doctor what she knew, which was very little.

Stacie mulled that over. "Some epileptics will fade into a coma-like state after a grand mal."

A grand mal seizure was something to behold, the convulsions taking control of the patient's entire bodily functions. Carol unclasped the microphone. "Previtt, was breathing interrupted in the seizure?"

"Not that I noticed. And he didn't make a mess."

A child began wailing inside a treatment room. Stacie started away, only to turn back and say, "Have them draw blood."

"They're only a few minutes out."

"Even so. Just in case."

Carol started to ask In case of what? But the doctor had already left. Carol passed on the instructions, then cut the connection and returned her attention to the waiting families.

Her next patient was a fairly standard case for indigent locals, a Hispanic male in his mid-thirties with severe abdominal cramps. Taking the patient's history, Carol learned he had been treating joint pains with ibuprofen and paying no attention to how many he took. Overdoses of ibuprofen over a long period could cause serious ulcers. With some patients, a pallid skin tone and serious abdominal swelling could be signs of a perforation, where the drug had eaten all the way through the stomach lining. This resulted in peritonitis, when stomach contents entered into the peritoneum, or abdominal cavity. This was a life-threatening situation and required immediate surgery. The patient was too dark-skinned, and his gut was too big, for Carol to make an instant diagnosis.

Both doctors were busy with urgent cases. Carol started for Dr. Henry, as usual. What she didn't want was to waste time on a tense night with the obvious. Before any diagnosis or course of treatment could occur, this patient required an ultrasound. In the past, though, Stacie Swann had insisted on checking Carol's work before issuing orders. But the waiting room was crammed and Previtt was inbound and it wasn't even midnight. Then Carol passed an open doorway and saw Stacie doing a verbal history while a child cried in a mother's arms. On a hunch, she knocked and said, "Got a young male, severe cramping, abdominal muscles tight as a rock, long-term abuser of ibuprofen."

Stacie did not even glance over. "Do his bloodwork, then phone upstairs and arrange for a scan."

"Got it." She returned to the patient and surprised him with her smile. She said in Spanish, "Everything is going to be all right."

Just after eleven thirty, Carol received a call from her husband. The sheriff asked, "By any chance, do you have another drug overdose?"

"Hold on a second." She walked over and shut the waiting room door.

Dr. Henry watched her return to the reception desk. "Everything all right?"

"It's Dewey." She put the sheriff on speaker. "Why are you asking about overdoses?"

She watched the doctor's features stiffen as he leaned in closer to the phone. Dewey replied, "We've caught rumors of something going down. Spent almost two hours chasing our tails. Just thought I'd check in."

Carol waited long enough to be sure the doctor had nothing to say. "Who is we?"

"Tell you later. Is that a yes?"

Their chief doctor hesitated, then gave her the nod. Tell him. Carol said, "Tell you the truth, we don't know what we've got. Previtt brought in a victim from the traffic accident out on 28."

Doctor Henry added, "There are no injuries that we can find, no contusions, head seems fine."

"That you, Doc?"

"Yes. And there are none of the aftereffects you'd expect to see with a grand mal."

There was the sound of the car's engine revving, and a muttered conversation, then, "Do us a favor and draw blood."

"We already have," Carol replied. "Twice. In the ambo, and again after we got him settled."

Dr. Henry added, "The crash victim or whoever he is still snores away in cubicle four. He refuses to wake up."

They heard another muted conversation, then the sheriff said, "Might be a good idea to put the patient in restraints."

Carol stared across the counter at her boss. "Did you just hear what Henry said?"

"Just to be on the safe side," Dewey replied. "We're about twenty minutes out."

Carol's husband entered the ER unit four minutes past midnight, accompanied by a stranger.

Carol's first thought was, this is the man for Stacie.

It was a totally woman's-intuition moment. No logical processing whatsoever was involved. But instinct played a solid role in ER work. When they had an unresponsive patient, vitals going south, a hundred possible reasons for the crisis, there was often time for just one action before the patient expired. Only after, when the trembling passed and she was safe in the staff room, would Carol often assign a logical reasoning to her decision. This ability of hers to make rapid and correct diagnoses was why Dr. Henry had insisted on Carol being head of his team. Perhaps it was his Caribbean background that made him so comfortable with her intuitive talent. All she knew was, he valued her ability so highly he had never found a need to even name it.

Dewey introduced his ride-along as Eric Bannon, down from Washington. Eric was rugged in the manner of a very dangerous man. He wore a navy jacket and knit silk tie and starched pinstripe shirt and charcoal slacks. But his dress was nothing more than a masquerade. Beneath the civilized veneer beat the heart of a guy who lived in the world of menace and threat. And did so with a feral calm. But unlike many of the patients they saw, this man lived by a moral code. Carol did not know how she knew. Nor did she care. Not just then.

Carol realized her stare was making the man uncomfortable. She did not care about that either. One thought dominated her just then.

She simply had to hook this guy up with Stacie.

Friday evening Sheriff Dewey Steen picked up Eric from the same slip road. They went first to the university's medical center, a vast complex that far outshone most of the central Florida town. The hospital's chief was a diminutive guy named Benny Benitez. He treated Dewey with casual disrespect and failed to pick up on Eric's name at all. Eric understood why Dewey had made this call first, so as to show how little help they could expect from Benitez and his team. Eric had seen this before, where a small town was basically seen as a parasite living off the money and power the university brought in. And nowhere was the attitude stronger than among senior medical staff.

They then drove north from town, down a darkened county road to the regional hospital. From the instant they entered the place, Eric knew this was ground zero. The chief nurse was Dewey's wife, a remarkably able woman for such a small county clinic.

The doors to the waiting room were closed. The loudest sound in the ER lobby was the glass entrance doors sighing shut as the ambo driver returned from a coffee run. The computer keys clicked as the ER internist, a very attractive woman named Stacie Swann, reversed the monitor time clock. Dewey Steen's belt creaked softly as he bent closer to the screen.

"Here," Swann said. "This is when the first patient woke up."

Eric could smell a faint fragrance to the doctor's dark hair, a floral shampoo and soap and the odors of a hard night. Stacie

Swann's intelligence held an intensity that seemed to vibrate in the air around her. Or perhaps it was just a mirage, the effect of how the senior nurse kept watching him. And smiling.

Carol Steen was a lean woman in her late forties, with a calm, knowing gaze. Her surgical blues were wrinkled and stained by her left shoulder. She wore a long-sleeved T-shirt beneath the top. Since their arrival, she had not spoken a single word directly to Eric.

The problem was, the monitor showed very little that could be directly tied to Eric's primary aim. The patient was clearly under the influence of some strange mix of drugs. But the claims the women made were not substantiated on the monitor. Eric watched as the nurse and Dr. Swann tried to stabilize the patient, and then she woke up and vanished. Eric asked, "No sound?"

"Can't," the doctor said. "Patient rights."

Dr. Henry came in twice while they surveyed the monitors. He appeared distracted, not certain whether he wanted to welcome them or even acknowledge their presence. He spoke with the young doctor once. The second time he went to the waiting room, drew out another patient, and vanished back down the hall.

"All right, I've seen enough." Dewey Steen straightened slowly. "And you're saying the blood didn't show you a thing?"

"We ordered a full toxicology work-up, standard for all suspected drug patients. It came back all clear."

Eric said, "If you can spare me a duplicate, I'd like to have my people take a look."

The resident doctor inspected him very carefully. "I thought you said you were a consultant."

"I am." Eric said, "But I can arrange for criminologists to give this sample a careful inspection and report back."

"I got the feeling there's layers to this boy he ain't letting on about," Dewey Steen offered.

"I'm working as part of a task force," Eric said.

"Looking at what, exactly?"

"That is classified."

Dr. Swann crossed her arms. "So are my patient's blood samples."

"I could get a warrant."

"Is this a joke?"

"Not at all," Eric calmly replied. "It's a threat."

Carol was searching for some way of easing the tension between Eric and Stacie when the crisis phone rang. Carol almost laughed out loud. Never had the phone's chirp sounded so welcome. She answered with, "Urgent Care."

"Carol, it's Rosie."

"Hold one." She told Dewey, "It's the regional operator handling the staties."

The sheriff settled his bulk against the counter. "Put her on speaker."

Carol waited as Stacie walked over, shooed the listeners into the waiting room, and slid the glass doors shut. "Go ahead, Rosie."

"The staties have a possible PCP abuser."

Carol knew Rosie well enough to trust her judgment. Carol's perspective was not shared by many of the local police. Rosie was a Latina in her early forties whose early beauty had faded to a hefty solidity. Even so, she tended to wear overtight outfits and flirt outrageously. Her husband, a local contractor that had done much of the interior work in Carol's home, pretended at a good-natured exasperation with his wife. But he adored Rosie's unquenchable Latin fire. Rosie was a passionate dancer and had twice been a finalist for the regional *Dancing with the Stars* contest. Rosie's current partner was none other than Previtt. Carol had previously thought the ambo driver would know nothing about music unless it came with a banjo and a kazoo. The first time she watched the two of them blister the dance floor with a samba had been memorable.

Rosie went on, "Highway patrol responded to a 911 because they had a car in the vicinity."

Dewey leaned his bulk on the counter. "Sheriff Steen here, Rosie. Where are we talking?"

"Between Sutter's Landing and the Felasco Preserve."

Which put the patient squarely in county's hands. Carol said, "Previtt is right here listening in."

"Hold one, I'll ask if they want an ambo."

While she waited, Carol scanned the monitors. It was an ingrained habit, done without conscious thought. Every cubicle was occupied, but things remained calm. Her gaze lingered on the accident victim Previtt had brought in. The young man was stretched out in the third cubicle, snoring so loud Carol could hear him from her station. He was well dressed in a nerdy fashion, cotton gabardine slacks and a pale blue linen shirt. His personal effects were in a tray on the shelf behind her and included a plastic pen pack, high-tech watch, and 430 dollars in cash. No phone, no ID. Carol was about to point out that lone similarity to the woman who had been brought in, when Rosie came back on and said, "I'm going to patch you in with the officer."

Stacie said to no one in particular, "I hate PCP cases worse than anything."

"That makes two of us," Dewey said.

Rosie came back with, "All right. Officer Wallace, go ahead."

"Ah, there's been a change at this end."

"Carol Steen here, Officer Wallace. County Hospital ER. We have an ambo ready to roll."

"That's a negative. Ambo not required."

"Sorry. I thought you were dealing with a PCP vic."

"So did I."

Stacie leaned over the counter. "Officer Wallace, this is Dr. Swann. Could you describe the victim's condition?"

"Ah, not really. No."

"Explain, please."

"I'm not...Look, this is going to sound crazy."

"We're all experienced ER personnel at this end," Carol replied. "We live with crazy all the time."

"I arrived on scene to find this guy going berserk. We're talking straight out of his head. There were four of us and we couldn't hardly keep the guy down."

Carol saw all the faces except Eric Bannon's tighten into scowls. She asked, "Sounds like a probable PCP to me."

"What I thought too," Officer Wallace said. "At first."

No one who had witnessed a PCP abuser go off the deep end ever forgot the experience. Six professionals often were required to hold them down. When the first cases began appearing in the early '90s, the ER staff had no idea what they were dealing with. The unfocused rage and the superhuman strength were unlike any other drug reaction they had ever seen. And suddenly it was everywhere. Toxicologists and pathologists around the country were comparing these freakish episodes. Everyone in ER work was accustomed to securing agitated patients. This was something else entirely, and the bloodwork was unlike anything they had ever seen. They knew they were observing the impact of a drug that could not be identified. It took almost a year before the data was collated and the substance named as phencyclidine, also known as PCP or angel dust. It took another fourteen months before the drug was ranked among the highest-danger category of illegal narcotics.

The officer went on, "Then all of a sudden, the guy just went quiet. I mean, totally still. Like he was dead, only I could hear him breathing. Pulse just got slower and slower. I know that sounds nuts, but I'm telling you, it was night and day."

Stacie said, "No, Officer, that doesn't sound nuts at all."

But in a way it did. Because one thing all abused drugs held in common was, they lingered in the system for a very long while. To have an abuser go from full-bore drug episode to calm was impossible. It was unheard of.

Only they had seen such an episode themselves.

Turning away from the mike, Stacie said, "We've got to check with other regional clinics, see if this pattern is showing up anywhere else."

"I can help with that too," Eric said quietly.

Carol watched Stacie shoot this strange man another look, then said to the mike, "Tell us what happened next, Officer."

"I decided we couldn't wait for an ambo. So I got the vic's brother to help carry him out to my cruiser. We were halfway across the front lawn when the guy wakes up. And bolts."

"He ran away?"

"*Flew* away, more like. I might've seen somebody run that fast before, like, in the Olympics or something. But not on all fours. And something else."

"Yes?"

"His brother tried to stop him. The guy *bit* him. And snarled. Like a, well, tell the truth, I don't want to say…"

"Like an animal," Carol said. The hairs on the back of her neck tingled. "Just like a wolf."

"You need to bring the brother in right now," Stacie said. "A human bite can be very toxic. He'll need immediate treatment."

"I'm rolling in five."

When Carol cut the connection, they stood in silence until Dewey asked, "You got any ideas about what we just heard?"

Eric Bannon opened his mouth, then closed it again.

"Go ahead," Stacie said. "You were actually going to offer something concrete here? Maybe answer a few questions?"

"I need to call this in."

"You do that," Stacie said, back to her former sharp tone. "While you're at it, why don't you get permission from whoever pulls your strings to let you tell us just what exactly is going on here."

"We're on the same side, Doctor Swann."

"Are we?"

"I'm here because we don't have many answers," Eric said. His gaze was as level and unfathomable as his tone. "But I'll ask my superiors to let me share what we do know."

His frankness silenced the young doctor. So Dewey said, "I'd sure like to be in on that chat."

Eric nodded. "I will ask that too."

Then Carol noticed movement on one of the monitors. "We've got an alert." Carol tapped the screen. "Our sleeper has just woken up."

Dewey and Eric Bannon remained in the waiting area because Stacie Swann ordered them to stay put. Which Carol agreed with, at least for the first few minutes. The ER cubicles were cramped and filled with equipment. Previtt followed them down the hall but remained poised just outside the doorway.

Carol's first impression was, the guy acted like a good drunk.

Of course, there was no such thing. Drunks were drunks. Unpredictable and dangerous. But some of them could cover a near-lethal blood-alcohol level with a very sleek veneer.

Most drunks were agitated and belligerent. They were savage fighters because their rage was unfocused and their natural inhibitions were doused in booze. A few, however, became very humorous, very engaging. Even so, a trained ER specialist knew within the first few seconds of an encounter that something was just a little bit off. Anything could trigger a shift from humor to rage. The danger still lurked beneath the smile and the happy words and the too-bright eyes.

And then there were the others.

Alcohol often revealed the patient's hidden nature. A normally placid individual could expose a streak of aggressive distress. Others, like the man watching them enter the room, became lecherous.

The man was in his late twenties. Carol guessed the patient's weight at around 250 pounds. Beneath the layer of blubber was a big-boned, muscled frame and remarkably long fingers. That was the first thing that struck Carol as she watched him fumble with the IV tubes. His hands and arms were long enough to reach across the bed, despite the restraints. "Don't touch those."

She used her sharpest tone, the one meant to subdue an entire waiting room of panic-stricken relatives. It had no impact whatsoever on the man. He gripped the three tubes and ripped them free, plucking out the needles. He did not even glance down.

His focus, his entire being, was directed at Stacie. There was an animal ferocity to the way his face constricted. An intent with no human emotion to it whatsoever.

The look held a predator's cold intensity, the casual savagery required to survive and kill in the darkest jungle.

"Previtt!"

"I'm here." The ambo driver stepped toward the bed. "You just hold tight, bub, else you want some of me."

The young man shifted around, the action drawing his entire upper body into a coil. He did not so much look at Previtt as take aim.

He snarled.

Carol's heart was racing so fast she could splice the seconds into a hundred shards. She backed up until her fingernails clawed the side wall and her body was between the patient and Stacie. She heard the chains rattle against the bed's railings and was filled with an illogical certainty that this patient could break free at any moment.

But this was *her* emergency room. And *no one* was going to threaten *her people*.

She screamed, *"Stay down!"*

Carol had the distinct impression the man did not understand what she said. But he swiveled his gaze so she was now the focus. Carol shouted, *"Now!"*

The man snarled once more. The fiercely brutal noise emerged from deep inside his chest.

Then he tore his bed apart.

When the two women started shouting, Eric debated whether he should ignore the doctor's order and head down the corridor. Then the place erupted.

A roar echoed down the hallway, along with the sound of rending metal. It was as though a multiple-car crash took place inside the ER.

The sheriff moved fast, Eric one step behind him. Even so, they had scarcely rounded the nurse's station before the man sprang into view.

He was a beast transformed.

The man wore bits of the bed attached to his wrists and one ankle. They made no difference whatsoever. He did not attempt to unbuckle the thick leather straps. Instead, the man reached down and *tore* the leather harness from his leg.

Dewey Steen snapped the catch to his holster. "Sir, put your hands where I can see them or—"

The man's roar was so loud it rattled the ER's front windows. He moved with impossible speed, leaping forward and gripping Dewey Steen by the throat and one thigh.

He hefted the massively built sheriff and tossed him through the front window. Like he would a doll.

Eric attacked.

He punched the man as hard as he had ever hit anyone, a straight right to the ribs, followed by another blow to the point where the jaw met the neck.

It felt like he was striking stone.

The man turned and swung his arm. Eric ducked as the metal bed railing whooshed overhead. He planted two lightning strikes to the man's gut. He might as well have been hitting a wooden training post.

The sheriff yelled through the shattered window, *"Get down, down, I can't make a shot!"*

It was unclear whether the man actually understood. The

response was more feral. He swept his head in an arc, snarling at the women, at Eric, at the sheriff's two-handed aim through the shattered window.

He leapt *over* Eric and flew past the sheriff…

And was gone.

They all stood and listened as the railing clanged and rattled on the pavement. Then, from a distance, they heard a wolf howl.

Eric waited while Dewey Steen was patched up and fussed over by his wife. The sheriff had multiple scrapes and bruises but nothing that required him being stitched up. Eric and Dewey were both interviewed by state patrol officers, who treated the report of a howling patient wearing part of a demolished hospital bed exactly as Eric would have, two months earlier.

When he was released, Eric asked Previtt, the ambulance driver, to take him back to the townhouse so he could report in on the secure phone.

Eric's boss heard him out in silence, then remained quiet for almost ten minutes. Eric had known the man for over fifteen years. He tried to recall another time when his boss had not come back immediately with an answer, an order, a grudging commendation, something.

Ambassador Reeves, former head of State Department intel and now advisor to the White House on matters related to national intelligence, finally said, "I have been ordered to stand you down."

It was Eric's turn to go quiet. He pulled open the rear sliding doors and stepped out into the first faint wash of dawn. "Say again."

"Orders have come in that you are to halt this investigation immediately. Your consulting contract is hereby revoked."

"Do you know why?"

"No idea."

"What about who's behind it?"

Reeves hesitated once again, then said, "My guess is the orders originated from across the river."

Meaning the Pentagon. "I don't understand."

"Think laterally. We're obviously not dealing with an issue that could be directly linked to anyone with stars on their collar."

"You mean, some military contractor is behind this?"

"I've said enough."

"So are you ordering me back to Washington?"

Once again, the old man remained mute.

Eric read the silence as best he could. "In that case, I think I'll hang around a while, take a little vacation."

"I think that might be a good idea. Reeves out."

Carol and Stacie stopped for milkshakes at a diner that during the school year was busy round the clock. Carol suspected the young doctor no longer wanted the treacly mix, but they bought them anyway. With Stacie following Carol's Tahoe, they drove south along Archer Road and into Carol's development. The dawn hour was spiced by a northwest wind, a rarity for late April. The high pressure dried out the humidity and turned the air crystal clear. Carol led Stacie back to a picnic table set well away from the house. The table was sheltered by a massive live oak. The branches creaked and the leaves whispered a soft welcome in the dawn wind.

Their home sat on a three-acre lot, the development's standard size. There was no one to hear them. Carol waited to see if Stacie was going to bring it up, or if she would have to. But when Stacie spoke, it was to say, "This is such a beautiful spot."

A pair of doves fluttered and hummed as they settled into the branches overhead. "It's why we love Florida living, mornings like this."

"What's that fragrance?"

"The orange groves to the west of us are in bloom." Carol hesitated, then asked, "Speaking of which, can I give you some advice?"

Stacie's gaze turned guarded, but she replied, "Sure thing."

"Lose the perfume. And switch to a shampoo without any fragrance."

"I didn't know either was that strong."

"The whole team notices. In a life-or-death situation, your power of smell could make all the difference."

"Duly noted." She sucked on her straw. "Can I ask you something?"

"Of course."

"The pharmacy records for Friday show you took out ocular antibiotics. Under my supervision."

Carol felt her face go red. "I shouldn't have done it."

"Why did you?"

"I asked. You brushed me off. As usual. It was an easy diagnosis. I apologize. It won't happen again."

Stacie set her cup on the table. "If it does, tell me after, okay?"

"All right." Carol studied the young woman, perhaps for the first time seeing beyond the attractive exterior. "Do you regularly check the pharmacy records?"

"At least once a week. Usually twice. I like to see what the other doctors have done in certain situations. And at my university hospital, a colleague had been abusing Oxycontin. No one had noticed it. I found he'd been dispensing opioids for everything, right down to the common cold. He supplied himself by making duplicate prescriptions."

Behind them rose a stand of loblolly pines. The treetops became brushed by gold fire as the sun rose over the horizon. Overhead the doves began cooing, a choir to the sunrise. This was Carol's favorite time of day. When everything felt right, and anything seemed possible. Even hope. She decided the time had arrived. "Do you want to talk about what we're dancing around?"

Stacie shook her head, "I don't even know where to begin."

"That makes two of us." Carol smiled. "When Dewey walked in with Bannon, I thought, you know..."

"Tell me."

"That you should hook up with him."

Stacie revealed a lovely laugh, bell-shaped and musical. "He'd fit right in with all my other male-type mistakes."

Carol's response was cut off by another car pulling into her drive. When Eric Bannon rose from the vehicle, she rushed over and demanded, "What on earth?"

"The sheriff told me I'd find you here and gave me your address. Is that Dr. Swann? Good, I need to speak with you both."

Stacie greeted him with, "If it isn't the secret agent man."

Eric stopped three paces from the table and said, "There is no easy way to say this. I need your help. As of an hour ago, the federal investigation has been shut down. There will be no assistance from Washington. They want this to disappear. May I sit down?"

He took their silence as consent and settled onto the bench's far corner, as far from Stacie as he could get and still be at the table. "When I first arrived here, Sheriff Steen told me he'd received a Washington-style runaround when he tried to report this issue. My superior only heard about it through a back-channel ally."

Stacie demanded, "Who is your superior?"

He met her gaze head-on. "I was sent down by a White House advisor."

"And now they've been shut down? You expect me to believe that?"

"There are powers who pull every politician's strings," Eric replied. "Even the President's."

"So who is pulling yours?"

"That's the problem," Eric replied. "We have no idea."

The long shift and previous day's emotional baggage left Stacie feeling as if she observed everything from a distance. Not to mention the lingering aftershocks from a patient who went wild on them.

Eric said, "I need to ask if I can count on you."

Carol turned to Stacie. "Your call, Doc."

The problem was, Stacie's mind had entered post-duty mode. She had experienced this often enough to know the symptoms by heart. Her thoughts felt congealed. The adrenaline high was gone, and all that was left was the ashes of bone-deep exhaustion. "We need answers," Stacie said. Even her words felt slow. Coagulated. "The problem is, I don't know what questions to ask."

"I know exactly how you feel," Eric said.

"Here's one," Carol said. "My husband's been trying to get Washington to wake up for three months, ever since this new drug first appeared. DEA responded with a huge yawn. DOJ, the same. Everybody wanted evidence. Which Dewey can't gather without help."

"Then I show up," Eric said. "And a day later, I'm called off the case."

"I'm thinking cover-up," Stacie said.

Eric settled his hands out on the rough-hewn picnic table. Thumbs touching. End to end, the distance had to be a foot and a half. "I can at least tell you what I *don't* know. Maybe that's the point at which to start."

Carol said, "Sounds good to me."

"There is no hard evidence that a drug called roulette even exists. Nobody has ever obtained a sample of the compound."

Carol said, "You battled the wild man in our lobby and you're still doubting its existence?"

"You're missing the point. We can't officially raise an alert without proof."

"Here's another question," Stacie said. "Who wants this to go away?"

He nodded, clearly approving. "That is an excellent question. And all the possible answers trouble my boss so much, he sent me down to investigate a rumor."

"It's more than that," Carol said. "Way more."

"That's right. It is." He looked from one woman to the other. "Will you help?"

When Stacie arrived at the hospital the next evening, Eric Bannon and the sheriff were talking with Carol Steen in the front lobby. Stacie parked so she could observe them through the sliding glass doors and remain unseen. She sat for a moment, wondering why watching the mystery man from the safety of her car would put such a zing in her breath.

Eric Bannon was an inch or so over six feet. No waist to speak of. Massive shoulders. Hair that some would call copper, but in fact was an interesting mix of several shades—blond and red and brown. Eyes to match, more golden than brown. Eric Bannon was quite possibly the stillest man she had ever studied. Like a big cat in khakis and a pale blue dress shirt.

She locked the car and crossed the lot. Eric spotted her and stepped through the ER entrance. He greeted her with, "Dewey's nephew has come through. There's another warehouse party scheduled for tonight."

"You sound like a doctor."

He tilted his head a fraction. "How's that?"

"Nothing extemporaneous. No need for greetings. Straight to the point."

He offered a quick smile, all the moment allowed. "Dewey says this is not common, three in a week."

"This close to the end of the school year, it sometimes happens.

But they'd vary the locations," Stacie replied. "Campus one night, nightclub rave in Orlando, beach party, Saint Augustine, then back. Like that."

"Tyler has agreed to vouch for me."

"Tyler is Dewey's nephew?"

"Right. Tyler Brock."

"Can I come?"

This time, his smile revealed a scar by his left temple, a hint of everything that had brought Eric to this point in time. Stacey had a sudden desire to reach out and touch it. Ridiculous.

Eric said, "Why do you think I'm out here talking with you?"

"Oh. I don't know. Maybe because you wanted to say how sorry you were for giving us such a hard time. Silly me."

"When does your shift end?"

"Not until three, but if it's quiet I can probably leave early."

Dewey came through the main doors and whistled. Eric said, "I'll swing by at midnight."

Carol followed Stacie into the medical staff's ready room. The lockers were metal and small and the tiled floor dated back to the clinic's earlier days, before the university's money transformed a run-down county clinic into a full-fledged regional hospital.

Carol leaned against the next locker and said, "So. You and the Washington secret agent man. Going to a rave. Together. Like, a couple."

"This is strictly business."

"Oh, please. I'm happily married to the best guy in nine states, and Eric Bannon still gives me butterflies."

"That is hardly a medical term." Stacie found herself struggling not to smile back. She conceded, "Okay, maybe he's not hard on the eyes."

"He's totally hot and you know it. If he dances as good as he looks, you're gonna need to get in line."

"Hey. We're going to investigate a serious issue."

Carol laughed. "I'll give you serious."

"Do you mind? I'm trying to get ready for shift here."

Carol remained where she was. "What are you going to wear?"

"What's the matter with what I have on?"

"That's a joke, right?"

Stacie disliked the nurse's smirk, and detested even more how it mirrored her own excitement. "I don't have time to go home. I'm already going to be leaving shift early."

"My daughter is almost exactly your size. I'll have her swing by with one of her outfits that gives my husband nightmares."

"You'll do no such thing," Stacie said, but Carol had already carried her smirk away.

When Eric pulled up in front of the ER entrance, Stacie was already dressed and making her final notes in the evening's files. She crossed the lot and opened the passenger door. Eric nodded a quick greeting, one professional to another, and raised a finger almost to his lips. Signaling for silence. Stacie quietly shut the door as the sheriff's voice came over the loudspeakers. Dewey was saying, "I'm worried Tyler might ignore my warnings and take himself another dose of that roulette."

"I'll try to stop him if I notice anything," Eric replied.

"Appreciate it." There was a pause, then, "We could just swoop down and roust the place. Bound to find all kinds of rats scurrying around once the lights go on."

Eric handed Stacie a handwritten set of directions and put the Jeep into drive. "We're not after arrests here."

"Speak for yourself."

"We need to know what the drug is, and where it's coming from."

"You get a passel of those guys under lock and key, one of them is bound to start singing."

"We'll try it my way first. You agreed."

"Wish I hadn't. You stay in touch, hear?"

Eric cut the connection and said, "You look very nice."

"Thank you."

"Anybody asks, we're an older couple meeting a young friend for a taste of what goes for the wild life in central Florida."

"What exactly are we looking for?"

Eric tapped the wheel. Once, twice. "The real question is, how much do you want to know?"

Stacie liked that. No attempt to shut her out, or play down her role. She liked that a lot. "I want to know whatever you can tell me."

"Last year at Burning Man a new drug popped up out of nowhere."

"You have agents at Burning Man?"

"DEA sends them in every year to scout the terrain. Very hush-hush. Because to be accepted there, they have to, you know…"

"Use."

"Right. Which means they are breaking about a dozen federal statutes."

"Unless they receive a special waiver," Stacie guessed.

"Which required them taking it all the way to the attorney general," Eric confirmed. "So five weeks after Burning Man, my superior was sent a top-secret report talking about a new drug. Roulette. Unlike anything they'd ever seen before. The high was extremely intense, but the downside was totally different."

Stacie liked how he paused then. Not testing. Giving her a chance to engage. "With most illegal substances, intense highs are matched by a specific set of potential side effects. Overdoses mean psychotic incidences, heart or liver failure, muscle contractions to the point where breathing becomes difficult."

"Right. None of that. Check the directions, aren't I…"

"This is your left coming up."

"Okay. So instead of the standard risks, roulette apparently impacts some people in totally wild ways."

"Wild is right." When he didn't say anything more, she asked, "That was why they brought you in?"

"No, I've never worked a drug case before." He glanced over. "At this point it all gets very confidential."

"Understood. This is your right coming up."

"My superior's name is Reeves. He contacted me because of how the agent reported that another group had sent observers."

"Who?"

"Defense."

"Get out."

"I told you, this is very—"

"Top secret. I heard you the first time. Military, really?"

"All I know is what I've been told. But for my boss to be personally involved usually means it's a solid. DEA reported that three agents from military intel were treated in the Burning Man clinic for overdoses of a drug no one could identify."

"But why would military intelligence have people there in the first place?"

"Which is exactly what I asked. Reeves thinks they're interested in the impact we've observed in the local victims."

"You mean, like, super troopers?"

"Okay, now we're into supposition. We're probably not talking about using this drug on just your normal soldier. This isn't aimed to heighten the ability of boots on the ground. But for the top echelon, highly trained specialists that go behind enemy lines in small groups, Reeves thinks DOD are trying out drugs that might heighten their stamina, speed, perceptive abilities. And for some reason, roulette failed."

"Wait, we're dealing with a drug that *didn't work*?"

Eric's features flashed into view as a car passed in the opposite direction. "It worked all right," Eric replied. "It just didn't do what they wanted."

Stacie had been to warehouse parties before. Some, not a lot. She loved to dance, and she found a secret thrill in edgy environments like this. Which made her choice in men all the more weird.

The few guys she had allowed close had all been so, well, tame. There was probably a better word, but that was what came to her here, standing alongside Eric Bannon. Her boyfriends had all been willing to let Stacie be the ambitious one in their relationship. Because she was more than driven. She lived for her work. She was intelligent enough to have recognized early on what this meant. Her relationships needed to take a back seat to her professional life. Most men disliked that intensely. They felt threatened. They felt this, they felt that. So during her second year in university, Stacie started telling guys exactly where they stood. And where she was headed. Stacie intended to become a standout internist, doing cutting-edge research on the next hot topic. And eventually land a senior position at a major teaching hospital like Boston or LA or Chicago.

The problem was, the men who'd accepted her drive and ambition were by definition passive. As in, willing to take a back seat in everything else. Either that or they were emotionally disengaged. Her last disastrous relationship being a case in point.

Shame about where all her careful planning had landed her.

She reached for Eric's hand as they slipped through the crowd, up to where Tyler waited by the front door. Eric's grip was hard as granite, and yet he held her with a gentleness she found oddly warming.

Eric was dressed in khakis with a military crease and an ironed knit shirt. Woven leather belt and Docksiders. His was probably the only shirt in the crowd that was tucked in. Stacie wore a sparkly top with a drawstring tie at the neck and waist over skinny jeans and sandals. She felt the humid night air touch her bare back and shivered.

Eric released her hand and moved over to Tyler. The young man was just as Eric had described, tall and massive and very nervous. The two bouncers by the front doors kept casting them looks. Eric motioned her forward, then spoke loud enough for the nearside bouncer to hear. "Hon, this is Tyler, the guy I was telling you about."

She flashed him a number-one smile. "It's so nice to finally meet you."

"Whatever." He smeared the sheen of perspiration on his brow. "I guess we better—"

"Just hold on. Now smile to the lady like you're really excited to be here with us." Eric turned his back to the bouncers and let his grin slip away. "Do it."

Tyler tried and almost succeeded. "Hey, this is great and all, but I'm ready to get this over with."

Eric laughed loudly and clapped the young man on his shoulder, steering Tyler around. "I don't know about you two, but I could use a drink!"

Eric played the cheery older guy doing his first ever warehouse event. Shook the bouncer's hand. Chatted with a trio of young ladies who were scoping him out. Kept Stacie close, touching her, smiling at her, saying over and over he wished he had not waited so long to come have this good a time, and hey, they weren't even inside. What did she like to drink, dance, how great she looked, her hair was fantastic, all the things an attentive date might say. Stacie stayed calm, smiling, showing him the quiet happiness that assured the bouncers they were just a couple out for a good time. Eric insisted on paying Tyler's entry fee, thanking him again for letting them tag along.

Just inside the first set of doors, he leaned in close like he was going to kiss her neck and said, "Did you see the ambulance parked around the building's corner?"

"Yes. It's not one of ours." Stacie leaned back and gave a very public smile. "Tyler is on something."

"I wasn't sure."

"Then you don't have much experience with recreational users, do you?"

Eric laughed gaily and carried his smile past the second set of bouncers. "None at all."

The instant she entered the chamber, Stacie was impacted by the wrongness.

All the warehouse parties she had been to shared a similar look and feel. The party area was normally a vast open space, surrounded by huge speakers and light machines. The patrons were handed glow tubes as they entered, sometimes also a drug, depending on the cover charge and how wild the night. Whether they took it was up to them. The floors were generally bare concrete, the walls graffiti-covered, and the air filled with CO_2 fog from the smoke machines. DJs were stationed on platforms from which they could lift the crowd to greater frenzy. Bars were long trestle tables with buckets of ice and booze.

The only thing this rave had in common was the music, loud and pounding. This warehouse was immaculate and done up like a nightclub. The dance area was built as a series of giant half-moon steps, lined by plastic pods in which professional dancers writhed their spray-painted bodies. Flashing lights timed to the music rimmed the dance areas and the bars, three of them, long as the walls. A vast upper deck extended from the rear wall like a metal tongue, filled with segmented lounges for the high rollers. Young people lined the stairs, excited and chattering, being allowed up top one at a time.

None of this made sense. The entire concept of a rave was to rush in, party, and flee before the law discovered what was happening. This place was too polished, too done up, too...

She turned to shout at Eric, but one glance was enough to decide he already knew. His features had undergone a drastic shift. Gone was the happy chatter. Stacie decided this was the expression of a warrior on foot patrol in Indian country.

She heard Eric yell to Tyler, "Where is the dealer?"

"You don't want to go anywhere near that guy. He's mean and his crew is worse." Tyler kept his back to the rear deck. "They're always up top. You know, so they can keep watch."

"You can't buy from the bartender?"

"Naw, it doesn't work like that."

Eric glanced at the long line of people snaking up the rear stairs, then turned away. "What about other dealers?"

Tyler wiped his face. "You don't understand nothing."

"Tell me."

"Anybody else tries to do business in here, see those guys in black standing by the upstairs railing? They make sure the dealers don't sell anything ever again."

"That makes your job easier." Eric handed Tyler three hundred-dollar bills. "Go buy whatever this will get us from Jerry."

Tyler looked at him, the fear raw. "Dude..."

"If anybody asks, we just want to try what we've missed out on until now."

"Did you not hear what I just said? Those guys—"

"I want you to straighten up," Eric said. "Do this and your job here is done."

Tyler swallowed hard, took the money, and started through the crowd.

Eric led her over to a table, then craned and waved at where

Tyler was climbing the stairs and joining the long line of young people. Eric gave Tyler a big smile and pumped his fist, evidently excited to get deep into whatever the people upstairs had on offer. Eric reached out and swept Stacie up in a one-arm embrace. "It'll look better if I go buy us a round."

Stacie disliked having him leave. She had a dozen questions she wanted to shout at him, a hundred. She liked his strength and vigilance there close at hand. Watching him slip away left her feeling exposed and underdressed and vulnerable. She forced herself to turn around and observe the dancers. She moved slightly to the beat, though she could scarcely hear the music over the pounding of her heart.

Chloe Harper despised her office. But she was required to camp here at all hours of the day and night. Her job demanded it. Despite the massive paycheck, if she had known how difficult it would be to remain exposed like this, she might never have left ops.

Chloe had spent her entire life in the shadows. Covert operatives melded with whatever cover was available. Survival demanded a talent for going unnoticed. Her office threw all these rules right through the four plate-glass walls.

Two sides of her corner office overlooked the Saint Johns River, burnished copper-gold by the lights along Jacksonville's RiverWalk. Two others faced the central bullpen and the ninety-seven cubicles assigned to all the corporate noncoms. Her desk was a slab of polished Brazilian granite, blue with red streaks. The custom ergonomic chairs were finished in matching blue leather. Most executives would consider it a throne room, especially as it was situated one floor below the owner's tenth-floor office suite. For Chloe it was just another cage.

She turned her chair to face the river and the shimmering cityscape. Most of the cubicles were empty, but not all. The cleaners passed up and down the corridor beyond her glass walls, studiously ignoring her. The company's CEO had denied Chloe the right to insert window shades of any kind. It was part of his policy of openness, even when the claim was a complete and utter lie.

Peter Sandling pushed through her door. The thick glass portal weighed almost four hundred pounds. The pneumatic hinges sighed softly in each direction, a sound Chloe had come to loathe. On a busy day the doors filled the bullpen with the sound of constant exasperation. As if the building was quietly disgusted with its occupants. "Ten minutes to one, I finally thought I was done for the day. Or the night. Ready to go home and open a good bottle of something cold. And what happens but I get your alert. I don't like alerts. Especially after the day I've had."

That was how her boss talked. Perpetually impatient. Like he had somewhere better to be, something more important that he needed to get done. Chloe said, "There may be a problem at the warehouse."

"Stage One or Two?"

"One."

"So this is only a sort-of emergency."

"We'll know soon enough. Jerry's due to call back in five."

Peter dropped into her visitor chair and began swinging it back and forth, just like a kid. The company's CEO was a boyish fifty with a mink-like frosting of grey in his very black hair. He exuded an energy so potent it infected the entire team. He wore round tortoise-shell glasses over dark brown eyes. Collegiate style clothes covered a lean frame that was never still. He was driven, intense, secretive, and one of two reasons why Chloe had taken this job. Money being the other. A lot of it, and more to come. If they were successful. Which she was determined to make happen. Whatever the collateral damage. She tolerated Peter's less savory personality traits because he shared her single-minded focus on results.

Chloe said, "Jerry thought he spotted another undercover."

"Cop or agent?"

"I checked with our contacts in Washington and across the Potomac. Everything's quiet. I'm thinking cop."

"Jerry is a total flake. We should have dumped him months ago."

"He's handled the Team One responsibilities well. The locals know him."

"He's still a flake."

"Jerry's team contains three of my guys. His number two is the woman I brought with me from covert ops. They'll take care of everything Jerry can't handle." Thankfully, Peter's retort was cut off by the chirp of her phone. Chloe said, "I ordered him to call back when he had photos." She hit the speaker and said, "Go."

"I'm sending you the pics you wanted."

She turned on her tablet and drew up the pictures. She saw a man and a woman, both in their late twenties or early thirties. Even from the odd angle of looking down on them, both had striking looks.

Peter leaned forward. "The woman is the doc?"

Jerry demanded, "Who's that with you?"

"One of my team," Chloe replied.

Jerry snapped, "We don't need any of Ryker's animals tearing things apart."

Peter snorted, shook his head, but did not speak. Chloe asked, "Do you recognize them?"

"The guy, definitely not. Probably a sheriff's crew. The woman, yeah, one of my guys says she stitched him up a while back. She's an ER doc at county."

"Hold one," Chloe said, and hit the mute. She told Peter, "The county hospital handled both the Level Two cases that got away from us this week."

Peter frowned at the photos but did not speak. Chloe turned the sound back on and said, "Go on."

"They came in with one of our, whatcha call them."

"Chrysalis."

"Right. Kid named Tyler Brock."

Chloe keyed the name into her computer and drew up the file. She swiveled the screen around so Peter could see. "The football star."

"Tyler claims he doesn't know nothing. But it's not just my stuff that's got him sweating."

"Wait," Peter stabbed the screen. "This kid's uncle is the sheriff?"

"We didn't know that at the time," Chloe replied. "You said bring in university joes and up he popped."

Jerry added, "I knew him already. Tyler was heavy into ecstasy in his off-season."

"Right," Peter said. "I remember now. And the cop is there because…"

Chloe nodded. She was tracking her boss now. "One of the cases that went to county did a bounder through the front window. Apparently the sheriff saw it happen."

"So he pressures his nephew…"

"Who he knows is a user into allowing a deputy and a doc to tag along." Chloe was used to finishing Peter's sentences. It was another of his more annoying traits.

Peter kept shifting his position. Back and forth. Like his body was set to a metronome's beat. "So now we…"

Chloe said to her phone, "Jerry, you know what to do."

"No problemo."

"Call me when it's done." When their guy clicked off, Chloe told her boss, "Now may be a good time for you to go play at deniability."

Eric had still not returned when Tyler reappeared. He leaned over and shouted into Stacie's ear, "There's a problem."

Stacie suspected the oversized kid was about to go into meltdown. He had either taken more of whatever he was on, or the drug had hit him harder. Tyler's pupils were severely dilated. Perspiration matted his hair and stained his shirt. His movements were jerky, almost robotic. "There sure is."

"Jerry asked me if you're cops. I told him no way, you were a doc and he's my uncle, but I don't think he bought it." Tyler risked a glance up top, then groaned, "Oh, man, he's watching us."

Stacie saw a lone guy standing by the upstairs balustrade, wearing a silk aloha shirt, with tattoos covering his arms and neck. "Did you get what we need?"

"He wouldn't sell me anything. You better clear out while you both still got legs."

"We need you to go buy us—"

"No, no way. I'm gone." Tyler leaned in close enough for her to catch his terror scent. "You don't get it. This isn't your clean little version of life. That guy up there will *kill* you."

Eric was still waiting for his order to be filled when he saw Tyler return down the stairs. He had been debating whether he should say something to the sheriff about Tyler's intake. Confidential informants dwelled in a grey area. They were generally granted a great deal of leeway when it came to personal behavior. So long as they did not harm others or threaten the investigation, agents tended to turn a blind eye. But Eric liked Dewey Steen and had seen first-hand the pain Tyler's behavior was causing.

Eric had handled a number of confidential informants and liked almost none of them. His first field mentor had classed working with Cis as just below herding goats. Cis tended to live in a constant state of crisis—crashed cars, raging infidelities, drug overdoses, bad debts—all superimposed on a perpetual diet of fear. Fear of exposure, reprisal, loss, death. Eric thought most of them had every reason to be afraid.

As Tyler rushed over to where Stacie stood watching the dancers, his expression was one of borderline terror. Eric's assumption that something had gone wrong was confirmed by Stacie's own flash of fear. But she recovered swift as a pro, smiling at the kid and trying to bring him down from whatever had happened on the flight deck. Tyler was having none of it, however. He snapped off a final remark and headed for the exit.

Eric remained where he was. He turned and gestured at the sweating bartenders like he was impatient for their drinks. If there was a danger, Eric doubted he could make it back to Stacie and then out to the exit before the alarm was raised. It would be easier to handle a threat if they were separated because it would split up the opposition.

Then Eric spotted the drifters.

The term was not much in use these days. Eric's first mentor had adopted it from his special ops days in Somalia. Drifters were assailants who never took direct aim at their prey. They moved in oblique patterns. To most people, including security, drifters remained merely part of the scenery. The only way to spot them was to watch the forest and not the trees. Study the entire group, and identify those who did not move in the random pattern of everyone else. Drifters normally operated as a unit, which made it easier for an experienced observer to track both their tactics and target.

This initial team of three focused on Stacie.

Eric remained where he was, hunting, until he spotted the second team. Eric assumed there was another staircase at the back of the deck, one which allowed the handlers to come and go in shadows. The second team formed a pincer movement, slowly making their way toward him. Eric assumed their tactic was to wait until he realized Stacie was threatened, then nab him when his attention was focused on the lady.

Eric picked up two random glasses from the bar, emptied one on the floor, wrapped his hand around it to shield it from view, and headed back. He allowed a couple to block his path, forcing him to the right. He remained careless in his movements, pausing long enough to smile at a passing woman. Eric raised the empty glass and pretended to drink. Just another partier out for a warehouse high. He shifted position as he did so, such that a passing couple shoved him further to the left. Fouling the aim of the drifters trying to close on him.

Then he saw one of Stacie's hunters grip her arms while another reached out and touched something to her shoulder. Eric assumed it was a miniature Taser, small enough to remain hidden until applied.

His hunters were sloppy. This was their terrain, their jungle. They were accustomed to taming rowdy partiers. At worst they probably assumed he and Stacie were undercover cops. Which meant Eric would be all about protecting his partner and shielding bystanders from harm. But Eric knew there was nothing he could do about Stacie until he first took care of his own assailants. Survival depended on Eric ignoring her plight, at least for the moment. That was the difference between a cop's training and Eric's own background.

Eric's first task was to eliminate the hunters tracking him.

Second, identify their controller and neutralize him or her before they could bring in reinforcements. Then he would go after the lady.

Everything else was secondary.

Eric pretended to jerk away from another couple locked in a sudden embrace. Then he drifted further left, apparently watching a slit-eyed young woman dance by herself at the crowd's perimeter. He looked upwards and smiled as a cloud of CO_2 drifted down from the overhead machines.

When the manufactured fog veiled their actions from any observers, Eric's nearest attacker closed in for the kill.

He had observed their methods when dealing with Stacie and was ready with a response. The assailant was a woman with a hard-edged beauty, good at her job and accustomed to having her smile momentarily disarm the prey.

Eric pretended to ignore her right hand and what it held. Instead he grinned broadly at her approach. Then he dropped both glasses and waved his left fingers inches from her face.

The woman's training worked against her. She flinched away so as to protect her eyes.

Eric's right hand jabbed the vulnerable cavity below her voice box. She froze in the sudden choking shock of losing the ability to breathe.

His left palm formed a hard flat slab and punched her nose upwards, shoving it toward her brain cavity. His right hand moved back eighteen inches and punched the ribs above her heart.

Her hand kept drifting up, but the brain was now swamped by pain. The muscles fired on adrenaline alone.

Eric caught her in a happy embrace. He danced her over to the nearest empty sofa and deposited her, but not before he stripped her hand of its weapon.

To his surprise, Eric did not hold a Taser at all.

Instead, he gripped an oversized felt-tipped pen.

Of course, it was not a pen at all.

Part of the report that had sent Eric south had focused on pens just like this. They assumed the tip exuded a single dose of the new drug. Tyler's claim that roulette was applied to the skin had confirmed this. Assuming this weapon contained the same drug, first came euphoria and an inability to connect muscles to the brain. This initial reaction happened in a matter of seconds. The victim remained relaxed and jolly no matter what was done to them. Onlookers simply saw a happy drunk.

Full impact required another ten minutes, by which point the heart rate slowed to twenty-five beats per minute and breathing was almost undetectable.

The initial report had also mentioned one side effect. The risk of overdose was extremely high, and almost always fatal. Three touches to exposed skin and the victim was gone. Permanently.

Eric touched the pen to the woman's neck and moved on.

But not far.

Eric stayed low, shifting far enough toward the room's center to be shielded by dancers. He kept his hands up and jerked to the beat, just another partier swinging to his own chemical music. All the while he held to a position where he could observe the woman.

The jungle was his now. The hunter had become bait.

He did not wait long.

One of the other hunters approached their partner, then a second. As they leaned over her, Eric moved in.

He touched the pen to the nearest neck and shot a lightning jab to the other hunter's kidneys. As the second assailant shifted into defense position, Eric applied the pen where neck met jaw. Then Eric danced back out of range.

The two attackers slapped hands to neck, their eyes round with shock. Eric let them see him. He wanted to watch their reaction to the drug now coursing through their systems. It was essential to saving Stacie. If that was still a possibility.

Their reactions would have been comic if Stacie's life did not hang in the balance. They both dropped their pens and reached for sidearms. Then their eyes filmed over. They fought hard, but could not defy the chemical bond.

As they slumped, Eric moved forward, pretending to laugh as

he supported them over to where they tumbled down on the woman. He kept laughing as he shifted them around, checked their pulses, and lifted one eyelid. He backed up, hands on hips, still laughing at them, then bent down and retrieved the two dropped pens.

He stayed low and kept moving, aiming for the trio carrying Stacie toward the shadowed rear exit. His best chance of saving her depended on not alerting any backup to the fact that he had survived.

He was midway across the warehouse when screams erupted behind him.

Which was when the controller spotted Eric.

The rear stairs were where Eric had expected. The railing and steps were all black metal, so they melded with the shadows formed by the upstairs gallery. The guy Eric classed as the controller stood out because of his bearing and his clothes. He was young to be in charge of such a professional crew, particularly one armed with highly specialized tradecraft. Which meant he was probably their leader in his own mind only. To the rest of his crew, the kid was just a puppet, his strings pulled by the real boss.

This guy was used to being noticed. He liked frightening people. He wore dyed blond hair in a punk Mohawk. His skin was heavily inked. Wristbands of leather and steel. Gun tucked into his waistband. He halted three steps above the ground floor, pointed at Eric, and shouted to his remaining crew.

The trio who had gone after Stacie handed her body to a man standing alongside the controller. Then they started back toward Eric. No attempt at subterfuge.

The controller and the guy carrying Stacie headed for the rear exit.

Speed was everything now. The three men tried to flank Eric. He let them approach from two sides and straight on, knowing the guns in their hands were worse than useless now, for if they fired they risked taking out their own team. Eric shuffled forward, pretending to take a boxer's stance, like he was hesitating over their massive builds.

Then he leapt straight up.

Eric gripped the metal bars holding up the gallery and aimed two spread-eagle kicks at the flankers. His shoes struck them from chin to nose. He twisted free of the rail, spinning his body as he dropped, putting his 211 pounds into a single blow to the third man's forehead.

He kept spinning, chopping the left-hand guy in the throat and the third attacker on his right temple. Back to the central guy, but there was no need for another strike. The attacker was already going down.

Eric raced through the rear exit just in time to watch the ambo peel out of the parking area and roar into the night.

After Chloe cut the connection, Peter showed no interest in leaving. "How are Ryker and his team?"

"Same as at our regular review two days ago," Chloe replied. She disliked intensely Peter's sudden decision to play commander-in-chief. But it was his company, his gig, his product. She decided there was no future in objecting. "In the green."

He picked up the tablet and studied the two intruders. "Run face recognition on the guy who's bothering your Jerry."

As she drew up the photographs on her computer, she said, "Ryker's itching for a chance to test his crew's limits."

Peter actually laughed. "I'm hearing the same tune from our DC contacts. I told them exactly what you need to tell Ryker. Bedlam and carnage is absolutely the last thing we need. Especially now."

"Good to know we agree on that point." Her computer chimed. She read, "No hit on the guy. Local or federal."

"What, he's not a cop?"

Chloe was not troubled by the absence of any data. "Some regional forces have deleted their clandestine operatives from all electronic files. Especially if they're going after the international cartels. There have been leaks."

"Just in case that's not it. Who could this guy be, exactly?"

"Might be statie."

"Or a fed who is deep undercover."

Chloe did not respond. She was thinking the same thing.

"Or maybe a relative of one of our MPDs."

"Too much of a coincidence," she replied. MPD. Missing and presumed. "We haven't had one in weeks."

Peter did a slow circle of the office. "Roulette carries a truth-serum phase. Tell Jerry to ask the guy what we need to know."

"Sure thing," Chloe said. Now was not the time to point out that Jerry tended to break his toys. Her phone rang. "It's Jerry. Hang on, you can tell him yourself." She hit the speakerphone and said, "Go."

The leader of Team One was clearly very shaken. "Ah, we got ourselves a problem."

Chloe said, "What are you telling us, Jerry?"

"The guy took out my crew."

When Peter circled back, Chloe held up one finger, silencing his outburst. "But you neutralized him, correct?"

"Ah. No."

"Say again."

"Me and Brad, we escaped okay. And we got the girl."

"Wait. You're telling me you *left him there*?"

Jerry's voice rose to a drill-bit shriek. "I'm telling you we barely got away!"

"Okay. Okay."

"That guy is lethal. He erased my whole crew in, like, seconds." Jerry's breathing rasped hard over the racing motor. "Your lady and her pair went after the guy while my three took on the doc. Your crew, they just *vanished*. So Brad and I loaded the girl into the ambo while the rest of my guys went after *this one guy*. He took them all out! We only got away because Brad had already started the ambo. I *never* seen anybody move like that."

Chloe coded in the combination and opened her drawer-safe. "Where are you now?"

"I just told you. In the ambo. We're taking the girl to the safe house."

"No, Jerry. You're not. You're going to turn around."

"Wait…What?"

"Stop and turn around. Do it now. I'm going dark. But you're staying on the line."

"This is *nuts*."

"Stay on the line, Jerry. And when I come back, I want to hear you're closing in on the warehouse."

When she hit the mute button, Peter said, "So maybe Ryker gets his wish after all."

Eric drove with his headlights off. It was a terrible risk, driving blind on a moonless night, racing along a county road he did not know. But the Florida country highways mostly held to straight lines. There was no traffic. The greatest hazard came from wildlife, deer and boar especially, who used headlights as their early warning system. But the alternative was to alert Stacie's kidnappers. Which would probably result in gunfire. And most likely end in Stacie's death.

The county north of Gainesville was hot, green, flat, and mysterious. The surrounding countryside was a semi-arid plain that produced more cattle than any other state except California. Eric had read up on the region before his arrival. His adrenaline-drenched brain sparked out such random thoughts as he flew blind at almost eighty miles an hour. It was times like this when he released the interior man from its tightly confining box. He preferred moving at such perilous speeds because it was only now, when death rode in the passenger seat, that he could ask why he did it. When he could confess that risk and sacrifice were the foundation of his existence. Times like this, he could accept the impossible and wish he had been born when knights errant still wandered the land. When it was considered both right and proper to risk everything for a good woman. When her next soft breath was the only thing that mattered. When logic and reason and strategy were all vanquished by the same four words: do the right thing.

Then up in the distance the ambulance's brake lights came on.

Eric slowed and halted in the middle of the road. He was almost unwilling to accept what he was seeing. The ambulance pulled onto the verge, and just sat there.

Eric waited with them. Moving forward on foot meant being separated from his ride. If they started up again he might lose them entirely. So he sat and waited, hoping the distance between the two vehicles kept them from noticing his presence.

Then the ambulance turned around. And started back.

Eric did not think. Or hesitate. He gunned the engine to redline and beyond. Then he slapped the car into gear. The Jeep's four-wheel drive gripped the rugged country asphalt and mashed him into his seat.

He raced straight at them.

His headlights were coming back on in three seconds...

Two...

One.

Chloe told Peter, "You're missing the point. Jerry is there as cover. The law is bound to check up, especially now that you want to accelerate the recruiting drive. They ask around after a warehouse gig and they hear about just another dealer. What they don't know is, three of my specialists are embedded in Team One."

Peter watched her take out the red phone. "So your guys…"

"Are extremely well trained."

"But this stranger took them out. All three of them."

"Right." She coded in the number for Team Two. When Ryker answered, she said, "We have a situation."

As long as Chloe had known Ryker, he had been an opera fanatic. He had also possessed the purest falsetto Chloe had ever heard. Ryker knew all the famous coloratura roles by heart—Handel's *Agrippina*, Verdi's *Alzira*, Strauss's *Ariadne auf Naxos*. His favorite was from Mozart's *Ascanio in Alba*, when he sang the role of a nymph who was also daughter of Hercules.

Lost. All lost.

That Ryker was gone now. And it was Chloe's fault.

Two years ago she had taken this gig and convinced her finest asset to come along for the ride. Ryker had been a specialist at the close-order kill. Stiletto, knife, poison, garrote, Ryker had been an artist. That too was gone.

Jerry had been right about one thing. Sending in Ryker's team meant mayhem.

Ryker, her former falsetto star, responded with a voice of rasping Sahara heat. "Define situation."

"A possible undercover operative has just taken out all but two of the first team. Jerry survived by fleeing the warehouse. The investigator, if that's what he is, remains on the loose."

"Not good."

"How soon can you go hot?"

"We're outbound now."

"Call as soon as..." Chloe stopped because Ryker was off-line. She cut the connection and sat staring at the phone. Nights like these, she missed her friend.

Peter drew her back into focus by asking, "Who's this Brad driving the ambo?"

"One of Jerry's loser pals. We had no choice about them. It was a package deal." Chloe resisted the urge to stand and pace. "Brad's not the issue we need to confront."

Peter started to ask, then it hit him. She knew because his face went white as old bones.

She said it anyway. "That unknown investigator is now probably in possession of multiple pens."

Peter slumped into his chair.

Chloe gave him a moment to sweat, then asked, "Can I bring Jerry back on the line now?"

When Jerry answered, he gave her sullen. "What?"

"Tell me you're on final approach," Chloe said.

"This is nuts, is what I'm telling you. That guy back there is a killer."

Chloe bore down hard. "Where are you, Jerry?"

"I've turned around, okay?"

She used her computer to draw up the ambo's tracker. "Jerry, you're three and a half miles out."

"I said I was going."

For once, Chloe agreed when Peter gave an exasperated wave of his arms. She said, "Team Two is inbound. When you arrive, identify the assailant but do not approach."

"Hey, no problem. That guy totally deserves what's coming to him."

"I'm going to patch Team Two in now."

"Uh, you said we can't have contact."

"That was before you let the guy go, Jerry."

"Hey. I didn't *let* anything."

"Whatever." Chloe hit speed dial on the red phone. When Ryker answered, she said, "I've linked this line in with Jerry."

Ryker said, "Jerry, can you hear me?"

"Not so good."

Ryker said, "Describe how the guy attacked."

"Fast, is how. I don't…" There was an instant's pause, then Jerry screamed, "Watch out, man, that's a car! *Car!*"

The phone's speaker gave off the blast of a horn and the sound of two men screaming. Brakes squealed. Then a crash.

Peter was leaning so close to Chloe's phone he looked ready to dive in. The sound of the wreck was massive, despite the phone's lousy speaker. A blast of noise resonated through her office. Broken glass and wrenched metal and more screams.

The cars separated, or so it sounded to Chloe. Two wrecks pried reluctantly apart. This was followed by the drumbeats of tires hitting the pavement. Jerry and the other guy were groaning now. And another voice moaned, this one female.

Chloe shouted, "Talk to me, Jerry!"

But the only reaction was the sharp shattering cymbal of another window being broken. Then a strong male voice called, "Stacie!"

Ryker murmured very softly, "Chloe."

She disconnected the two calls and murmured, "Here."

"Unlink my phone from Jerry's."

"Already done."

"Do you have a fix on the ambo?"

"Roger that." She checked the GPS tracker on her screen. "Highway 58, mile post sixteen."

On the other phone's speaker, a woman moaned once more. The guy responded, "I have you. Everything's fine now. Let me get you out."

The woman named Stacie managed words for the first time.

"My arm."

"Hang on, you're tangled. Okay, here we go. Let's get you our of here." There was the sound of a body being shifted, then footsteps scrunched over glass, and faded.

Through the red phone Ryker said, "Our ETA is twelve to fifteen minutes."

Which was too long. Much too long.

Then Chloe heard footsteps returning over the rubble, louder and louder.

Chloe found herself tensing, as though the next blow was aimed at her.

Over the speaker Chloe heard another body being pulled from the wreckage. Jerry screamed, "My leg! My leg!"

The guy said, "I want to know who arranged this."

"Man, didn't you hear me? I'm hurting!"

Peter's head was almost touching Chloe's. He whispered, "Wire it to your computer speakers, hit record, and up the gain."

Chloe grimaced. She should have thought of that. The sound now resonated through her office as Jerry let out a long low groan.

The guy said, "There's the easy way and the hard way. What's your name?"

"Jerry."

"Okay, Jerry. You tell me what I need to know and I call the authorities and they dose you with all the meds you can handle. Which is a lot, right? When is your backup due?"

"Man, I don't know…" The words choked off.

"The hard way, Jerry, is very hard. I load you and your pal into the rear of my Jeep, which is still running, hear the engine? And I drive you somewhere dark. And we talk all night."

Jerry moaned, "What do you want to know?"

Peter sighed. "That's it. We don't have any choice."

Chloe was already reaching into her drawer-safe. "Roger that."

Peter drew the keyboard around and started typing. "I hate

this worse than anything."

Chloe drew out what appeared to be a third phone. "Worse than prison?"

Peter grimaced and kept typing. "Jerry knows too much, right?"

"He knows enough." Chloe keyed on the device. "He knows me. He knows the company. He knows about Team Two. He knows the production—"

"I have the ID." Peter sighed. "What a mess."

Chloe had already decided they had no other option. But choices like this required as much shared blame as possible. "Read it out."

Eric squatted in the glass-strewn rubble. He knew he ran the risk of being spotted by a passing motorist. And he needed to get Stacie to the hospital. She did not appear injured, but there was no telling what internal damage she might have suffered. Plus the drug was still in her system, they needed to draw samples, they needed to monitor her behavior, they needed...

Eric remained there beside the supposed leader. Jerry's left leg was most certainly broken. His fancy silk shirt was shredded. His face and both arms were bleeding. "Who is your handler?"

"I don't get names. Come on, dude, make the call."

"When we're done." Eric held to a calm, soft tone. "We've got all night, long as it takes."

Jerry groaned.

"You've got a name, right? A contact. Who supplies you with the drugs? And the pens? All this is really interesting to me, Jerry. Answer my questions and we'll get you all fixed up. But first I want to know the chemical makeup of your drug and where it comes from."

"I can't..." Jerry's eyes widened. He breathed easily for the first time since Eric had dragged him from the ambulance. "Oh, wow. That's way better."

"Focus, Jerry. Who's your contact?"

Jerry's eyes dilated as swiftly as the two attackers touched by

Eric's pen. Faster. He slurred softly, "Man, this is great."

"Jerry, talk to me. What's…"

He stopped talking because the guy was no longer there. Jerry released a long sigh. And was gone.

There was no reason why Chloe should have difficulty finding air for her next breath. She was not the one whose tracker had just been sent the signal. Even so, her mouth gaped open and she panted as they listened to the guy say, "Jerry? Jerry!"

Peter started working the keys. "Okay, I've got Brad's signal-code."

Reluctantly, Chloe forced her fingers to lift the phone linked to her teams and their tracker-signals. The device had a little skull-and-crossbones design done up in fake diamonds on the right-hand corner. A bit of gallows humor that now came back to bite her.

Peter read off what sounded like just another telephone number. Sent from any device but this one, the number would ring twice and disconnect. It required an underlying pulse to respond. When it did, the GPS tracker embedded in the wrist of each crew member emitted a toxin that halted both breathing and heart in fifteen seconds.

When she hesitated, Peter snapped, "Wake up over there."

Chloe slammed the kill-device down in front of him, rose, and walked to the window.

Peter huffed an exasperated breath. But when he picked up the phone, he hesitated. Chloe watched his reflection in the city nightscape. Peter held the device in one hand, the other poised to code in the number. But he couldn't do it.

She came as close as she ever had to actually liking her boss at that moment.

Then over her computer's speakers she heard the footsteps scrunch back across the glass, approaching the ambulance. Closer and closer.

When they could hear the guy breathing into Jerry's phone, Chloe walked back to her desk, took the device from Peter's lifeless fingers, read the number off Brad's confidential file, and coded in the number.

There was the sound of a body being shifted. The guy said, "Come on, talk to me."

Chloe hit send.

This time there was a soft moan, then nothing.

The silence gripped them both.

Then a scratching sound filled the room, followed by soft breaths. The guy had picked up Jerry's phone.

Peter demanded, "Who is this?"

There was a moment's hesitation, then the guy responded, "You first."

A woman's voice called faintly from the distance. The drug slurred her speech, but the name was unmistakable.

"Eric?"

The phone went dead.

Stacie was protesting even before she was loaded onto the padded gurney. "I don't need to be strapped down."

Previtt fitted the leather bands around her wrists and ankles, then another across her lower ribs. "All part of the service, Doc."

If Stacie even noticed how the ambulance driver, his assistant, the sheriff and two deputies all watched her, she gave no sign. Her focus stayed exclusively on Eric. "You should use the gurney for the other victims and let me ride in front."

"No need, Doc," Previtt replied.

"Both are DOA," Sheriff Steen replied. For the third time.

Previtt shifted around to the gurney's head and nodded to his assistant. "On two. One, lift."

"Eric, make them stop."

He disliked how she was swamped by this urgent need to get up, move around, take control. The frowning intensity of her expression disturbed him. She had said nothing about having been drugged back at the warehouse. Or kidnapped and transported out here. Or how she was now surrounded by patrol cars and flashing lights and officers in uniform.

All Eric said was, "Carol is waiting. You'll be checked over by…"

"Dr. Henry," Previtt offered.

"Right. You'll have a good rest, then tomorrow night—"

"Eric, no."

He stepped in close enough for his face to completely fill her field of vision. "I want you to listen very carefully. You've probably suffered a concussion on top of a drug that we don't know anything about."

"That's absurd. I feel *fine*."

"I'm glad to hear it. Now I want you to behave. You hear me?"

She lifted her head far enough to see the leather straps and the metal chains that held her arms to her sides. "I *hate* this."

"You need to chill, Stacie." When she kept struggling, Eric asked, "Do you want Previtt to give you something to relax you?"

"He wouldn't *dare*."

But she did stop fighting the restraints. Eric remained where he was, watching her argue with him through the ambo's rear window as it pulled away.

When the lights faded in the distance, Dewey Steen said, "Walk me through what happened."

The sheriff wasn't asking him to describe again the wreck and the two corpses now bagged in black plastic. Dewey wanted to know about what went down back at the warehouse. Their patch of official turf was rimmed now by flares and state patrol deputies with waving lights. Because the county road had no alternative route, the few cars that passed were walked down the verge then waved away. Otherwise the night was theirs.

When he was done, Dewey asked, "You're saying this place was built up to be something more than a simple rave."

"It was finished up like a nightclub, right down to the two DJs and women in cages."

One of the deputies muttered, "That just don't make no sense at all."

Dewey looked over but did not speak. They continued their slow route around the ambulance and his wrecked Jeep. "You took out how many of those jokers?"

"Three in the first attack, three more by the rear exit."

"Remind me not to get you riled." Dewey held the plastic bag containing one of the pens up to the light. Eric saw no need to mention the other two pens he had in his pocket. Dewey asked, "Did Tyler take another dose of this stuff tonight?"

"I doubt that very much." Eric described watching Tyler hustle back down the stairs, terrified and in a hurry to escape. Which was immediately before the two teams went into action. He hesitated, then added, "Stacie suspected he was high on something when we arrived."

Dewey kicked at the rubble. "My guys report the warehouse has been cleared out. Nothing there but the same old mess you saw after the last party."

"Any word on Tyler?"

"He hasn't come home, is all I can tell you right now. We put out an APB. I'll alert his school in the morning."

"Then I guess we're done here," Eric said. "I want to go check on Stacie."

"What's left of your ride has to be impounded." He gestured to one of his deputies. "Jack here will give you a lift to the hospital. Call me soon as you hear something from your people."

They made the drive in silence. Faint hints of the coming dawn washed the eastern sky as the deputy pulled up to the hospital's main entrance. Eric entered by way of the ER. Carol was there waiting for him, with the news that the initial blood tests had come back negative and Dr. Henry had given Stacie a sedative. Eric told Carol the bare minimum, then insisted on seeing the patient.

Stacie looked so vulnerable lying there strapped to her bed, and so beautiful. Eric asked if he could stay with her a while. He expected an argument, but Carol merely pulled a blanket and pillow from the closet shelf. Eric allowed himself to be tucked into the recliner. The last thing he saw was Carol's smile as she cut off the room lights. He fell asleep to the sound of Stacie's breath.

Eric woke just after eight. Stacie had not moved. He checked her restraints, then stood looking down at her. Her dark hair was spilled across her pillow, framing a face as lovely as it was pale. Her lips were slightly parted and a sheen of perspiration covered her forehead. He knew a sudden urge to kiss her. The thought was so ludicrous he let himself out of the room.

Carol was off duty, but the day nurse clearly had been alerted. She let him use the hospital's phone, as his own had been lost at some point during the night. Eric called Reeves and gave a preliminary report. The nurse then brought him a breakfast tray. When he was done, she led him to a vacant room and brought him a razor and a set of hospital blues. Eric showered and shaved and dressed, then returned to Stacie's room and settled back into the recliner.

The night's events drew from him a familiar pattern of response, as though the fourteen months that separated Eric from his last case did not exist. He visually walked himself back through the entire episode. He kept his eyes open throughout, because watching Stacie endure the night's consequences actually brought him a more intense clarity. When he was done, Eric began a mental list of the factors that needed further investigation. After a time his mind gradually drifted away, back to other unsolved cases, and the mysteries he carried with him still.

He had never regretted leaving the agency. The bureaucratic infighting and the paperwork and the mind-numbing red tape and the competition caused by too many agents chasing too few advancement slots, all that was permanently behind him. The only reason Eric had agreed to return to action was because he answered only to one man, the superior he had most admired and enjoyed working for.

Unlike Eric, Ambassador Reeves thrived on the competition between agencies. He was a master at winning the Washington battles and took special pride in protecting his subordinates. Reeves was brutal when an agent underperformed. But for those few who met his expectations, Reeves prided himself on being the best boss any of them would ever know.

Eric was going through the next possible steps when he glanced over and saw Stacie's eyes were open. "You're back."

She pried open dry lips and whispered, "I've never slept with a guy on a first date before."

He was filled with a sudden urge to wrap his arms around her. He made do with fitting the straw into her mouth. She watched him with a childlike intent as she drank. Then she asked, "How much was real?"

"Enough." He carried the empty cup into the bathroom, refilled it, then fit on the top and returned to the bedside. "More?"

"Not right now." She had lifted her head and was inspecting her restraints. "Have I, you know, bugged out?"

"No."

"That's not a very medically correct term to use."

"I'd say it fits the moment perfectly."

"They drugged me, though. Back at the warehouse. That happened."

"It did. Yes."

"I need to rest. Will you stay with me?"

The question touched him as few things had in a very long while. "I'll be right here."

Her gaze opened. It was a womanly thing, this ability to say so much in silence. She watched him for a long moment, then sighed and passed into slumber, easy as a trusting infant.

Eric stayed there watching her until he too fell back asleep.

When he awoke, her eyes were open once more. The sun had shifted so that it fell directly on her face, illuminating golden filaments in her dark gaze. He asked, "Should I close the curtain?"

"Please." When he returned to his seat, she asked, "What time is it? Better still, what day?"

He checked his watch. "Just after three on Sunday afternoon. Do you need anything?"

"More water. And..." She used her chin to indicate the bathroom.

Eric helped her drink, then pushed the call button. When the nurse appeared, Stacie repeated her request. The nurse checked her vitals, then asked Eric if he'd wait outside the door. He stood in the hallway, listening intently, hearing nothing except water running. He allowed himself a shred of hope that her dose had been too small to create anything like what they had both witnessed.

Fifteen minutes later, the nurse opened Stacie's door and invited him inside. Stacie was back in the bed, hair still damp from the shower, face scrubbed, wearing fresh hospital blues.

Belted to the bed.

The nurse asked if she was hungry, then said the doctor would be with them shortly. Stacie waited until the door sighed shut to reply, "But I am the doctor. At least I would be, if they'd let me go."

Eric had no idea what to say, so he remained silent.

She lifted one arm as far as the restraints allowed. "Are these necessary?"

"I have no idea. I hope not."

He expected Stacie to demand her release. Instead, she seemed to find comfort in his lack of certainty. She asked, "Will you tell me what happened?"

"I'll tell you everything you want to know."

The straightforward response seemed to pacify her even further. She settled back onto the pillow and shut her eyes. "Have you been here the whole time?"

"I left to shower and phone Washington. Otherwise, yes, here by your side."

"Have I, you know…"

"You've been asleep. Calm. Totally fine."

Her face creased with the effort required not to break down. When she was calm once more, she said, "It means a lot, having you stay."

"If I were in your position, I'd feel exactly the same."

"Can I ask you something personal?"

"You can ask me anything you like."

"Are you married?"

"I was. She died."

"I'm so sorry. When?"

"Seven and a half years ago."

"What happened?"

Eric had no problem with her questions. What they had been through broke down most barriers, as far as he was concerned. "Extreme PKD."

"Oh, Eric."

Polycystic kidney disease was one of the nation's most prevalent genetic disorders and also perhaps the least well known. Impacting one in every five hundred Americans, PKD resulted in cysts covering the kidneys to the point where a transplant was necessary. In the most serious cases, known as autosomal dominant, the cysts grew into a forest that covered the entire abdominal cavity. Death in such cases was almost inevitable. "Thanks."

"What happened after?"

He stretched out his legs. Took his time reflecting.

"I'm sorry, I don't have any business—"

"No, it's fine. Really. I was with State Intelligence at the time. It's the smallest of the nation's intelligence agencies. Ambassador Reeves ran it like his own private fief. I quit to take care of her that last year. Reeves handled it as the sort of dismissal he'd give a wounded agent, so I could keep my benefits. I hated resigning, but it was the right move. Assignments had kept me away from her a lot during our married life. I didn't want her to be alone during those final months."

"You did the right thing."

"I took night courses and got a degree in forensic accounting. After she died, it was easy to slip into that work. I could lose myself in the numbers."

"Take time to heal," she said. "And then?"

"Four and a half years ago, Reeves came calling. He had taken on a White House advisory role. No title, but he liaises between the President's chief of staff and all the intelligence alphabet. Reeves was looking for a lone wolf, someone he could trust in situations like this."

"Wow. Have you ever met the President?"

"No. Neither the interest nor the desire."

"Oh, come on."

He liked how easy the smile came. "What, you think I'd make that stuff up?"

"No, it's just...the White House."

"Yeah."

"So where have you been?"

"I worked a project for Reeves in Libya. And another in Syria and Jordan."

"All the global garden spots." She tasted the words several

times before asking, "You never wanted to give marriage a second go?"

"I guess...Sure." Eric took his time maneuvering through the verbal mine field. "Not many ladies are interested in a guy who puts his life on the line."

"Unofficially."

"That only makes it worse. I date. Some, not a lot. Mostly first dates."

"I believe I've sung that tune myself," Stacie said.

He nodded. "I've been trying to stay busy."

"Then this Reeves guy sends you down here."

"Right. And we go raving."

"And I wind up a patient in my own hospital. Chained to a bed. Waiting for the hidden beast to take over." She looked down at the restraints on her wrists. "Would you go see what's keeping the doctor?"

But as Eric rose from his chair, Carol walked in. She was dressed in civilian clothes and wearing makeup. Stacie thought the change somehow rendered the woman both lovely and vulnerable. As though dressing up somehow stripped away the shield every ER specialist was required to wear. Carol asked, "How are you feeling?"

"Trapped and ready to escape," Stacie replied. "Where's the doctor on call?"

"Hiding. Dr. Henry's taken personal charge of your case. He's on day shift next week and is off duty until Monday morning. He wants to keep you here one more night."

Stacie understood the delay now. If she had been in Dr. Henry's position, with the ER's front window still covered by cardboard and masking tape, she would probably have done the same thing. Even so, she started to protest, "Carol, please go bring the locum—"

"No. Absolutely not. Dr. Henry's right and you know it."

"I'm not going to bug out. I took a shower and dressed all by my little self, well, watched over by the same nurse who strapped me back in here." When Carol remained stationed by the foot of her bed, she added, "Eric, tell her."

"It's not my call," he replied, but gently. "Or yours."

She rattled the chains linked to her arm restraints. Eric reached over and gripped her hand. "Steady."

Carol's gaze showed a merry gleam. "Dr. Henry wants the lab to check your blood again. The reports have come back totally clean so far."

"Go ahead. It's not like I'm doing anything important here."

"You're healing," Eric said. "Recovering. Resting. That's important."

Carol drew another three vials of blood. Casting little glances at the hand Eric held while she did so. Stacie was waiting for the nurse to say something so she could jump all over her. But all Carol said was, "Your meals should be here any minute now."

"Are you actually going to feed me?"

"No, honey. We'll release one arm and Eric will stay right here to make sure you behave. Won't you, dear?"

"I'm not going anywhere unless you or Stacie say otherwise."

Carol gave Stacie a round-eyed look of mock astonishment, then left. Stacie said, "She's awful."

"I like her."

Carol returned with two trays. She wheeled the tray over in front of Stacie, raised the back of her bed, then said, "Eric, be a dear and unstrap her right arm." She watched them eat for a moment, then left and returned with a second chair. She settled on Stacie's other side and said, "The ER's quiet. Will you tell me what happened?"

"I'll go one better. Can I borrow your phone? I lost mine last night." Eric set his tray on the floor, took her phone, and dialed. He placed it on the bedside table and touched the speaker. As it started ringing, he said, "The voice you'll hear belongs to Ambassador Reeves."

Stacie felt a rush of excitement. "Your boss in the White House? For real?"

"As real as it gets," Eric replied.

A harsh male voice came on and barked, "Who is this?"

"Eric again. Borrowed phone."

"Are we secure?"

"The phone belongs to one of the hospital staff." He asked Carol, "Is the room miked?"

In response, Carol rose and walked to the door and touched a switch. "Monitors are off."

The phone demanded, "Who is that?"

"I'm joined by the two ladies I told you about. Carol Steen, chief ER nurse, and Dr. Stacie Swann."

"Is that wise?"

"Yes, in my opinion," Eric replied firmly. "And necessary."

A pause, then, "Very well. Has the victim revealed any aberrant behavior?"

"That's a definite negative."

There was another pause, this one longer. Eric held up one finger, halting any desire Carol might have had to quip. Finally Reeves must have reached some decision, for he said, "All right. I've checked on the pens you described. Discreetly. My contact was forced to take her query to others. They in turn demanded to know where she had obtained the items. No matter how quiet they claim to keep this..."

"For you to have obtained them during an unofficial investigation will raise any number of red flags. Could your source tell you where they came from?"

"The manufacturer is a group called Palindrome." Reeves spelled the name. "They are a privately held group based in Jacksonville. Their original revenue source was generic pharmaceuticals. Palindrome has since become a primary supplier of several key drugs to VA hospitals. But my source says the size and scope of their research contracts are completely out of line."

Eric glanced at the women. "Which probably means the company holds contracts with Defense Intelligence. They use the VA research grant as a cover."

"That is my take as well," Reeves said. "My source was extremely concerned by the prospect that these implements have been used on American soil. She insisted that she be shown any hard evidence I might have. She wants direct contact with you. I refused, of course."

"Your ally is going to alert her superiors," Eric said. "And they're going to widen the alert."

"The clock is ticking. Find out what you can and depart. Reeves out."

The night passed in shared harmony. Eric did not restrain Stacie's right wrist. She did not protest again. Instead she simply insisted on holding his hand. Eric shifted the recliner around to where he could stretch out in parallel to her bed. He slept like that, her hand curled up inside his own, almost like she was doing with her fingers what she could not do with the rest of her. He slept and did not dream.

The next morning he was awoken at dawn by Carol arriving with clothes from his townhouse. He stood sentry while Stacie used the facilities, then showered and changed and listened to the two women's voices on the other side of the bathroom door. There was a calm familiarity to the moment, a sense of peace carried over from the previous night. He heard one of the women laugh, and hoped it was Stacie.

He slipped downstairs and bought a new phone from the hospital gift shop, loaded it with a thousand minutes, then returned upstairs for breakfast. When they had finished eating, Eric and Carol left the hospital together, heading for the University of Florida's main medical campus. Carol said, "I'm perfectly capable of driving myself."

"I know you are. Will your husband meet us there?"

"I told you he would." She turned to face him, and said, "So. You and Stacie."

Eric should have handled the comment better than he did. But he could still feel the one-armed embrace she had given him as they had departed. And the warm lips that had gentled his cheek. Soft as the breath of thanks she had offered. Rich as the look. Another one of those amazing glances, so deep he was still falling. "I need you to tell me what's going on with her."

"Oh, please."

"What?"

"Don't you even *think* of claiming that your interest in the woman is totally professional." She pointed to the intersection up ahead. "Turn right."

He studied her. Carol was all lean muscle and well-defined features. "You remind me of my late wife."

Her smile vanished. "Stacie told me about that. I'm so sorry for your loss."

"Her family farmed in western Maryland, not far from the Appalachian Trail. It's some of the most beautiful country I've ever seen. You remind me of the folks I met there." He glanced over once more. "There's something about a country lady's smile. Big as the night sky."

"Why, Eric. You old charmer, you."

He said again, "Tell me about Stacie."

"What do you want to know?" Her smile resurfaced. "Mind you, I will need to strip away all the stuff she wouldn't want me talking about. What's the word you secret agents use?"

"Redact. And secret agent no longer."

She laughed. "Right. This after us listening to you chat with the White House."

"Back to the subject at hand," he said. "Stacie strikes me as an extremely capable doctor. Very sharp, very focused."

Carol nodded. "You're thinking she's too good for our little country clinic."

"That's not what I meant."

"Yes, it is. Left turn coming up." Carol swiveled back to face front. "The answer is, I don't know very much. A few months back, Dr. Henry got a call from a friend at the Gainesville medical center. The university hospital knew we had an opening. They had a resident internist who was looking for a chance to do some ER work. Dr. Henry says her credentials are extremely impressive."

"Will you ask around?"

"Of course, Eric." She smirked. "And I can pass her a note at lunch, if you like."

"I'll hand her my own notes, thank you very much."

"That's the main building up on your right. So...you think maybe somebody might come after us?"

"We just need to be careful." Eric pulled into the parking lot and reversed into a spot from which he had a clear view of the entrance. "Where is the genetics lab?"

"Third floor of the wing to your right."

"This is the only way in or out?"

"For visitors. All the other doors require a hospital ID and code that's changed every couple of weeks."

"Okay, get out your phone, please. I want you to put my number on speed dial."

As he gave her the number, Carol typed it in, then repeated it back to him.

"The first hint of trouble, you alert both me and your husband. You don't wait, you don't assume you can handle whatever it is."

Soon as Chloe heard from Ryker, she phoned Peter and told him Carol Steen and their mystery man had arrived at the UF medical center. She would have preferred to handle the situation on her own. But the company CEO had called her nine times the previous day, insisting on updates she did not have.

Peter entered her office a few minutes later. The company's CEO did not look like he had slept at all over the weekend. Chloe had managed a few broken hours. Not nearly enough. Her dreams had been repeatedly shattered by ghost whispers from Jerry and his sidekick, Brad. She had never cancelled the lives of her own operatives before, no matter how inept. The fact that it had been absolutely necessary sounded good in the safety of her glass-lined cage. But throughout Chloe's too-quiet Sunday, the guilt had etched her every breath. As Peter seated himself, Chloe phoned Ryker and put him on speaker. "What's your latest?"

"The ER nurse entered the UF medical center alone." Ryker's voice sounded like Chloe felt, dry and rasping and utterly disconnected from the peril. "The guy who took out Jerry's team is just sitting there in his ride. Watching the doors."

She addressed both men. "My primary Washington contact finally reported back an hour ago. His name is Eric Bannon. Officially he's a forensic accountant."

Ryker said, "Wait, we're worrying about a civvie?"

"It's a cover," Chloe replied. "Bannon was with State Intel for nine years, mostly in the field. He left seven years ago. Officially, his file is closed. He consults, he lives a quiet life, end of story."

"He's still in the game," Ryker said. "Bound to be."

"Correct. Bannon is now handling assignments for one Ambassador Theodore Reeves."

"I know that name," Peter said.

"He is a White House advisor on intelligence activities."

Ryker said, "Not good."

"Terrible," Peter agreed. He leaned toward the phone and asked, "Ryker, could your team take him out?"

Chloe shook her head. "That is an extremely bad idea."

But Ryker said, "Absolutely."

"And remain unseen?"

"Peter, just think for a minute—"

"No problem," Ryker said. "The guy's looking in the wrong direction with the sun in his eyes. We can slip in using the surrounding cars for cover, do the job, and vanish."

"No guns."

Ryker's laugh sounded dry, disused, grave-like. "I'm here with the entire Team Two. What's the point of guns?"

Peter turned and gave her the hand. Silencing any further protest. He said, "Do it."

Chloe sighed.

"Roger," Ryker said. "Moving out...Wait one."

"What's wrong?"

"County patrol car just pulled up in front of our guy. Yeah, it's Steen. He's rising from the car, Bannon has joined him. They're talking. Now they're going inside together." A beat, then, "We could do them together."

"No," Chloe said, taking back control. It was, after all, her office. Her team. Her ops. "Stand down. That's an order."

As the two men headed toward the hospital entrance, Dewey asked, "Carol in there?"

"She is, yes. She has a friend who's a biochemist. She's agreed to take another look at our blood samples."

"Lauren. Sure. Great lady. Appreciate you driving Carol over."

"It's probably not necessary. Broad daylight and a public place like this. But still."

"I'm a belts and suspenders kind of guy, especially when it comes to family."

They entered the lobby's cool wash and Eric directed them to a quiet corner. "Did you ask this hospital about any transitions like what we saw?"

"I like that word. Transition." Steen was big-boned and calm and steady. His response was measured, his expression calmly intent. "Of course I asked."

"And?"

"My contact in the university security brought in one of the head ER docs. The lady didn't actually come out and say it. But you could see what she was thinking."

"That you're just some hick cop with a wild story picked up at a little country clinic."

"Yeah, that pretty much sums it up."

"Any word on the drug in those pens?"

"I've just got off the phone with the state lab," Steen replied. "They say it's something called, hang on, I wrote it down." He slipped half-moon reading glasses from his shirt pocket. "Labellan. It's licensed as an animal tranquilizer. Patents are held by a company over in Jacksonville called Palindrome."

"You don't say."

"What, you know them?"

"First time I heard that name was this morning in Stacie's room." He recounted the conversation with Ambassador Reeves.

"That's a remarkable coincidence, you hearing about it from your Washington folks and me getting this news from the lab," Dewey said. "I hate coincidences worse than a double shift."

"Tell me about Labellan."

"The drug is used mostly in the wild. One dose will knock out a bull elephant."

Eric said, "The lab results on Stacie came back clean."

"Fast acting, fast to dissolve into your basic amino acids," Steen confirmed. "After that, only place to actually find concrete evidence is in brain tissue. The only reason the lab knew about it is, it's been tied to several regional date-rape cases. Two recently arrested suspects carried doses in eyedroppers."

"We need to get access to those case files," Eric said.

"Already put in a request with the state." Dewey pointed to the reception desk. "Let me go see if my contact can spare us a minute."

Eric watched Dewey cross the hospital lobby. He liked how the sheriff had time for everyone, addressing the receptionist and a nurse and a passing doctor and a cleaner with the same laconic warmth. Dewey maintained a balance of distance and approachability. Beneath the surface was a piercing intensity that Eric thought would make the sheriff a formidable interrogator.

When he returned, Eric said, "I want to lay something out for you. The way we've been thinking is based on how the evidence we've got suggests we caught an isolated incident."

"Two of them," Dewey corrected.

"Right. Two partiers who bugged out after overdosing at warehouse raves. But what if we're looking at this all wrong? What if we've actually just caught a glimpse of the dragon's tail?"

Slowly Dewey scratched the stubble on his chin. "Interesting."

"Let's suppose just for a second that your clinic was not the first to witness these incidences." Eric pointed down the hospital's main corridor. "That a number of them have come in. Right here. And up to now everything has been kept totally quiet."

The sheriff continued to drag his fingertips up and down his jawline. "An ER center this big, you'd be talking about a dozen folks keeping a secret. Maybe more."

"Actually," Eric said, "all you need is one."

The fingers froze. "The pen."

"One ER doctor or nurse or maybe even a staffer," Eric said. "On duty every time they have a rave where the drugs are sold. With just another pen in their pocket. Ready to administer a calming dose at the first sign of alarming symptoms."

"But the highway patrol officer described his incident happening long before they showed up at the clinic."

"An aberration. If they are testing this drug of theirs on a number of subjects, some are bound to get away."

"And you're thinking this because..."

"Remember the vehicle I wrecked," Eric said. "They have their own ambulance. Or they did."

"With their own driver," Dewey said.

"And their own pens," Eric said.

"So this drug..."

"First thing Tyler said about roulette was, the effects change. At the time I assumed it meant an uncertain set of responses. What if it's a gradual alteration over multiple doses?" Eric gave that a beat, then asked, "Do you have an ID on Jerry yet?"

"Jerry Adams. String of arrests up Savannah way, starting when he was eleven. Two stints in juvie, one in state for possession with intent. Two years ago he dropped off the map. Nobody I spoke to was surprised to hear he died under suspicious circumstances."

"And the other guy from the ambo?"

"Brad Hatterly. Born in Orlando, never strayed far. Multiple drug-related arrests. I got both their files in the car. Back to roulette. How do you tie this to the two corpses we carried to the morgue last night?"

"The coroner took blood and tissue samples, correct?"

"He said he would." Dewey checked his watch. "They're due to start on them about now."

"Have him search the skin of both victims for a scar in an identical spot. There should be evidence of an exploded capsule in the subcutaneous tissue."

Dewey took out his phone and got busy texting. "Anything else?"

"We need to find their contact inside the hospital. Which will require somebody going through the ER duty records."

Dewey finished texting, pocketed his phone, and pointed toward a narrow-faced African American heading their way. "My pal in security might give us a hand with that."

Carol and Lauren Crane had been best friends since high school. Lauren was exactly the same now as then, only more so—intelligent, highly capable, passionate about science, and utterly no-nonsense. She had played basketball and run track through college, but with a casual attitude toward both that had set her coaches' teeth on edge. Lauren loved the sports, just as she loved to fish with her husband and two sons. And she loved to ski. And dive. But she *lived* for her lab.

Carol entered the UF genetics lab and confronted a state of chaos. "What's going on?"

"One of the generators blew just after midnight. I got a call from security at four this morning. A passing janitor noticed liquid seeping under the door." Lauren plied a mop around three technicians squatting by a series of metal cabinets. "We lost six containers full of tissue samples."

One of the technicians offered, "We're almost ready to replace the unit."

"That's just great," Lauren said. "Then you can start logging in all the work that's been ruined."

Carol asked, "What about the samples I sent you?"

"Gone. All of them. I don't know what else to say except I'm sorry." Lauren pointed them toward the door. "I hope it wasn't anything critical."

A glass half-wall separated Lauren's lab from the one next door. A lumpish guy stood on the wall's other side, a lab gnome in dark-rimmed glasses, almost translucent hair and bad complexion. The guy leaned in close, as if trying to hear Carol's response, "Tell you the truth, I don't know what it was. We had symptoms in two patients that just didn't make sense. We were hoping you might be able to suggest something."

Lauren asked, "Can you get us more samples?"

Carol watched the lab geek's forehead come to rest against the glass. "Hard to say."

Lauren steered her towards the exit. "Let's get out of here. I haven't eaten since forever."

As they reached the door, the technician called over, "I found the problem. A wire worked loose here. The generator's probably fine."

"Dr. Benitez ordered it replaced," Lauren said.

He hit a switch and the cabinet emitted a soft humming. "You sure about that?"

"What Benny wants, Benny gets. And he says, replace the machine. Keep that one as backup." Lauren ushered Carol out. "You know where to find me."

The university medical center's dining hall was one of the areas that Carol most liked about the hospital. It was located in the building's oldest wing but had recently been remodeled with patients and staff in mind. The large area was segmented with plants and light and half-walls so that people enjoyed as much privacy as any vast chamber might offer. She and Lauren took their trays to a glassed-in patio area that overlooked the interior garden. Noise from the other tables surrounded them like a soft waterfall.

Carol stared at Lauren's tray. "What on earth are you eating?"
"Don't you start."
"What is that stuff in your salad?"

"It's called ancient grains. You should try it."

"Does it come with pulled pork?"

"My daughter got me on this. She's studying sports nutrition at UCF. She says it will increase the likelihood of my holding our grandbabies."

"I'm not sure it's worth it. What are those white flecks?"

"You know perfectly well that's feta cheese."

Carol let her eat a few bites, then said, "I need to tell you something."

"So tell. You'll be amazed to hear I've learned to eat and listen at the same time."

"This is highly confidential. As in, nobody else in the hospital can know." Carol started with the first patient going wild on them. She took Lauren right through to Stacie waking up strapped to the bed and two body bags in the county coroner's fridge.

Lauren had long since pushed her tray to one side. Now and then she picked up a morsel with her fingers, all without taking her eyes off Carol. "You think the mess in my lab wasn't an accident."

"I know it. Well, I don't know, as in, hard evidence. But yes. I'm sure somebody on the hospital staff wanted you not to inspect those samples."

Lauren must have seen it in Carol's face, because she did not ask. She declared, "You have more tubes of Stacie's blood."

"In Eric's car. Drawn every six hours. And more taken from the two dead guys."

"And Eric is…"

"The secret agent. Former agent."

"Who had you listen in while he talked to that guy in the White House."

"About the pens. Right."

Lauren leaned across the table and did a teenager's version of a mock whisper. "This is just so totally cool."

"Tell me."

"Here I thought you were withering on the vine out there in cow country."

"Life is a thrill a minute."

"So why are we still sitting here?"

"Because," Carol said, "I need to know about Stacie."

Trey Bower, Dewey's contact in the hospital's security system, ushered them through the monitoring station and into a windowless office, where he motioned them into seats. As he slipped around his desk he asked, "This a courtesy visit?"

"Not a bit of it." Dewey sketched out what they knew, hesitated, then asked, "You understand where I'm headed?"

Trey had stopped typing and now sat facing the two men. "You think somebody on the ER staff is helping a drug-maker hide their dirty laundry."

"Maybe," Dewey corrected. "Perhaps."

Eric spoke for the first time since sitting down. "If they are, the clearest indication would be an ER staffer who is on duty every time there has been a recent rave."

Trey's brown-black gaze had not shifted off Dewey. "Man, what you're asking, if it's real, it's radioactive."

Eric said, "Think about what Dewey just told you. His country hospital, well off the grid, gets two cases in one week. I'm down here from Washington because rumors are swirling about a new drug hitting the central Florida rave scene. Gainesville is reportedly the epicenter, but the university medical center has never had a case?"

Dewey said, "You know what they say about coincidences."

Trey turned to his keyboard. "You got the dates of recent

raves?"

Dewey handed over a slip of paper. "Every rave for the past two months where we received an alert."

Eric said, "This needs to stay secret."

"Man, secret doesn't cover it." Trey typed at lightning speed. "I should be wearing a bomb disposal suit."

Lauren told Carol, "Stacie Swan was one of my all-time favorite people. As you've no doubt already learned, she's a first-class doctor. But she and the hospital director, you know Benitez, right?"

"Well enough not to like him."

"See, I always knew you were a good person. Stacie caught him being a total skunk and went public. Or tried to..."

Carol watched her friend's face go from animated to stone. "What's the matter?"

"The man himself just walked in." Lauren's gaze was stone hard. "What I'd give for a chance to shave him down another few inches."

Dr. Benny Benitez, El Comandante to his many foes, was a former thoracic surgeon who had risen through the administrative ranks to become director of the university hospital. He was short and wore shoes with platform heels and fought a constant battle with his weight. He liked to portray himself as a charmer, with the big Cuban smile and the loud hello to everyone who might further his aims. But among the hospital staff, Benny liked to bark. He forced his lower-tier employees to live on the perpetual edge of joblessness. Turnover among the non-medical ranks was constant. Doctors mostly escaped the worst of Benny's legendary rants. Nurses avoided him at all costs.

The trustees and administrators, however, loved Benny Benitez. They ignored what they referred to as misdemeanors. They did not care about his poor staff relations. Because Dr. Benny had one quality that shone so brightly it blinded them to all his many faults.

Benny Benitez brought in the big donors.

"He's coming our way." Lauren's gaze would have melted lead. "There's never an Uzi around when you need one."

Carol disliked the look of genuine rage that creased her friend's features. Talking about their mutual friend had torn open a very real wound. Lauren risked her job if she met the dictator bark for bark.

"Lauren, what are you doing here? Don't tell me you left those technicians up there unmonitored!"

Carol halted her friend's response by nearly leaping to her feet. "It's my fault, Dr. Benitez."

"And you are?"

"Carol Steen." Benny disliked having to look up at Carol. She could see it in his face. So she rounded the table and gave him a big smile as she stepped nearer. "I asked Lauren to meet in hopes that you might be able to offer me a job."

He danced back a trace. "Lauren didn't mention anything about this to me."

"Actually, sir, I blindsided her. I know your hospital doesn't currently have any openings. But I wanted to get my name on the list, you know, just in case. There's nothing in the world I'd like more—"

"So what are you…What's your name again?"

"Steen, Dr. Benitez, sir. Carol Steen."

"So what, you're another lab technician?"

"Actually, sir, I'm chief nurse in the county clinic's ER department."

The news shook him. Carol was close enough to see the tense shift of his gaze, the electric bolt. "Wait…Stacie Swann, she's…"

"Oh yes, how nice of you to remember. Dr. Swann is our new resident."

Benny Benitez backpedaled. "All applicants for new positions have to go through proper channels. Lauren, I want you upstairs monitoring those technicians and making sure they don't destroy any more samples."

"Sure thing, Dr. Benitez."

Carol stood there by the table, ready to wave cheerfully if he glanced back. But Benny Benitez scurried through the doors and vanished.

Lauren relaxed in stages. "Girl, that was one stellar performance."

Carol pretended to pat her hair. "I could do better with a little rehearsal time."

"We're talking Oscar quality. May I have the envelope, please?"

Carol seated herself and said, "You were about to tell me how your beloved leader had something to do with Stacie's departure."

"He had *everything* to do with it. Oil and water, those two."

"Tell me," Carol said. "Don't you dare leave out a single dirty detail."

Almost an hour after Dewey and Eric entered the security room, Trey cut off his computer and said, "No single ER employee, from doc to janitor, was penned in for all those shifts."

Dewey asked, "What about widening the net to include the entire hospital—"

"Won't help. Expanding the search to eleven hundred employees in any combination would lead to dozens of suspects."

Dewey thanked the young man, and they left the security station. As they walked down the hall, he said, "Trey is solid. His family's seriously messed up. He grew up armed with every possible excuse to go wrong."

"He doesn't strike me as a guy looking for excuses," Eric said.

"You got that right." Dewey headed for the elevators. "Come on, I want you to meet Lauren, see where the real work gets done around here."

The last hour of Stacie's imprisonment was by far the worst.

Dr. Henry stopped by to say he was waiting for the results of Stacie's latest blood tests. Assuming they came back clean, she was to be released. In the meantime, he left her right hand free so she could eat.

If only she had an appetite.

Stacie could not stop the tidal rush of memories. Staying busy had always been her best weapon against the clamor of so many bad moves. But now she was strapped to her bed, and Eric was off playing secret agent, and the room became crowded with her two greatest foes. Guilt. And regret.

Stacie had selected the University of Florida's medical center for her residency because it had offered her the chance to double specialize. Urgent Care had only recently become a recognized branch of hospital medicine. Stacie was attracted by the lure of making a strong impact in a relatively new field. But she was also drawn to a new and innovative approach taking hold in internal medicine.

There was a growing trend among some newly licensed doctors. They wanted to move away from the standard rifle-shot approach to a patient's problem. Instead, this new breed thought a patient's latest health issue was best understood and treated when combined with long-term care. Which meant spending a great deal of time on a patient's history, diet, attitudes, and so forth.

This was in complete opposition to the immediacy of ER work, and yet for Stacie and many young specialists, this approach framed the trend of future medicine. Stacie wanted to combine the two. Deal with the urgent, then focus on the long term. UF had granted her the chance to put theory into action.

Put simply, Stacie Swann lived for her work. Or rather, she had. Until she lobbed a grenade at her own career.

Three months before finishing her residency, Stacie had discovered that Dr. Benitez, the hospital director, was having an affair. With a nurse trainee, a young woman assigned to Stacie's ER team.

Stacie had been incensed at the idea of a man in his position taking advantage of a student who was almost exactly one-third his age.

She had taken it to the board.

The board responded to her accusations by threatening to fire her.

Stacie then hired an attorney to represent her for wrongful dismissal.

Two days later, she received a phone call from a senior trustee. She had treated his daughter after a severe asthma attack. The man and his wife had tearfully vowed to remain in Stacie's debt forever. Even so, the hospital board member told her, "Walk away."

Stacie had difficulty believing she actually heard him correctly. "Benitez is in the wrong here!"

"And I'm telling you it doesn't matter."

"I'm going to make him pay."

"You can try. But all the big guns are on his side."

"He plays around with one of my girls, and the board is going to let him get away with it?"

"That's right, Stacie. They are."

"That woman is young enough to be his *grandchild!*"

"And I'm telling you there are things at work that you don't understand."

"I don't care!"

"You should." There was a conspiratorial lowering of his voice. "Look. Benny Benitez doesn't have that job because he's a saint. Do you know how much he's raised for the medical center in the past two years? A hundred and ten million dollars. Do you really think the board is going to let that man go over an infraction like this?"

"We'll see," she replied grimly.

"You go forward with this, and you're done. Let it go, and you can walk away with your head high and your career intact."

The proceedings got very nasty, very fast. Innuendos began spinning through the hospital community. The hospital's chief pharmacist, one of Stacie's closest friends among the hospital staff, told her she'd heard rumors that Stacie had been caught stealing. Then came a report from one of her fellow residents that security suspected her to be behind a recent theft of opioids.

Before this erupted, Stacie had fielded offers from three of the nation's most prestigious teaching hospitals. Now they stopped accepting her calls.

Six weeks later, the same board member approached her with a final offer.

Stacie was granted a tiny cash settlement in exchange for signing a nondisclosure agreement. She was not to request a recommendation because one would never be forthcoming. Which effectively spelled the end of her dreams of medical stardom.

By that point, Stacie was utterly exhausted. Defeated. She caved.

Now Stacie lay trapped in the bed of a county hospital. Every sound from beyond her door plucked at the raw wound to her heart. Her ambitions lay crumpled in the room's shadows. Voices drifted in from the nurses' station. Their laughter burned at her. She might love her work, but she hated being relegated to this county outpost. All because she had done the right thing. Hearing the staff's friendly banter only made the fury burn hotter.

Dr. Henry knocked softly, then opened her door. He smiled down at her and announced, "The tests came back clear again. Ready to go free?"

She wished she could come up with something clever in response. But just then the acid of regret was so strong she could scarcely manage a nod.

Carol was still fuming over Stacie's treatment when her husband and Eric Bannon entered the hospital cafeteria. Lauren noted the anger in her gaze and said, "Carol, there are laws against gunning down a hospital director."

"I've got a friend on the force. He'll get me off." She pointed to the two men coming through the main entrance. "Maybe Dewey will loan me his gun. That'll make it official. Sort of."

"Who's the hunk with him?"

"Eric."

"The White House secret agent guy? You didn't say he was good looking."

"I like him for Stacie."

"You know, for once, your idea isn't half bad."

Carol rose as the men approached and said, "Hon, you remember Lauren."

"Sheriff, you need to lock your wife up for murderous thoughts."

Dewey eased himself down with a sigh. "I don't even want to hear what that's about. Eric Bannon, meet Lauren Crane, one of my wife's best buddies. Lauren, this is Eric."

Lauren asked, "So what's it like, being a super spy?"

Eric seated himself next to Dewey. "Next time I meet one, I'll ask."

"We came in here hunting bear," Dewey said. "All we got is skunk."

Carol said to Lauren, "I believe that's my husband's way of saying he needs our help."

Dewey asked, "How much does Lauren know?"

"I told her everything that's happened. I needed to, if we're going to ask her to enlist."

"I'm in," Lauren said. "I don't know what I'm into yet, but if it means going after El Comandante, I know all I need to."

"We don't have a shred of evidence to take aim at anybody. Much less the hospital's chief." Dewey turned to Eric and said, "I trust the lady and so does my wife. But this is your call."

"We definitely need help," Eric replied.

Dewey said, "Okay, we got a couple of half-baked ideas and a lot of unanswered questions." Dewey explained what they'd come in looking for, an ER employee who was on shift every time they'd recorded a major rave. Eric tag-teamed then, explaining the lab results had come back on the pen, identifying the drug as Labellan, a licensed animal tranquilizer manufactured by Palindrome. Eric passed around the evidence packet as he did so. Carol liked seeing the two men together, shoulder to shoulder in comfortable tandem. It gave her a surge of very real pride. Her husband mixing it up with an agent down from the big city. Going after the bad guys.

When they were done, Lauren announced, "Palindrome is a big donor to this hospital."

Carol felt herself caught by the same spark that both men showed. "My husband is not a big one for coincidences."

Dewey asked, "What do you know about them?"

"Not a lot. All these big pharmaceuticals are very hush-hush when it comes to their research. Everything goes through Benny's office." Lauren clearly enjoyed being the center of attention. "They're working on something related to the blood-brain barrier. I know that much because their lab is next to mine."

Carol said, "The creepy guy works for them?"

Lauren grinned. "Say the word, I can arrange an introduction."

"Tell me about this barrier," Eric said.

"The blood-brain barrier is a semi-permeable membrane that separates circulating blood from the brain's extracellular fluid. It's formed by endothelial cells connected by what are known as tight junctions. The barrier allows the passage of water, some gases, and lipid-soluble molecules by passive diffusion. Very little else can get through, except for glucose and certain amino acids that are crucial to neural function."

Dewey looked at Eric. "You get all that?"

Eric rose to his feet. "I need to make a call."

Eric walked back through the main lobby and exited the hospital. He liked the open sky for a backdrop. During his wife's two-year decline he had known more than his share of bland hospital corridors and muted conversations and quiet misery. He shut his eyes and enjoyed the sun on his face for a moment. When he was ready, he placed the call.

Ambassador Reeves answered with, "Tell me you're making progress."

"We have fragments, sir. But fitting them together is mostly guesswork at this stage." Eric outlined the findings from the state lab, then the news that Palindrome was a major source of funding for the UF hospital. Last came the idea he'd shared with Dewey about a plant inside the hospital. He finished with, "Sheriff Steen has an ally in hospital security. We checked the roster against the known raves. No ER employee was on shift for all those events."

Reeves's response was immediate. "Then you need to look higher up the food chain."

"Unless I'm wrong in my analysis."

"There are too many coincidences at work here. You're not wrong."

"In that case, our contact at the medical center suspects the hospital director. But luring him into the open would be tough. Dr. Benitez is too well insulated."

"What about pressuring the university with the evidence you've gathered?"

"We have established no definite link between Palindrome and any illegal event. Whoever's keeping their secret are specialists at removing loose ends."

"The same seems true of Washington. I am being stonewalled," Reeves said. "I am open to suggestions.""

"The only solid lead we have at this stage is Palindrome."

"Contacting them would signal the watchers that you are still on the case."

"Sir, I think we should assume they already know."

Reeves gave that a beat, then decided, "Very well. But I will make the call. An official query from the White House might keep you alive a little longer."

Which of course was why Eric had phoned Reeves in the first place. "Thank you, Ambassador."

"Time to poke the hornets' nest. Reeves out."

Peter entered her office just as Chloe's encrypted phone rang. She touched the connection and said, "Hold just a second, Ryker." She muted the call. "Yes?"

"Something's come up." He shut her door, pointed to her phone. "Where is he now?"

"They're still shadowing Bannon and the sheriff."

"Good." Peter slipped into the chair opposite her desk. "I've just heard from Washington. Ambassador Reeves has made an official request for Palindrome to host Eric Bannon. Reeves got his ally on the Senate Appropriations Committee to phone me. Personally."

She felt the air around her congeal. "What?"

"He contacted somebody outside our loop, Chloe. Which means he's at least partly aware of Palindrome's involvement, and our connection to the guys across the river."

"Our Pentagon contacts must be in a total panic."

"They deserve nothing less." He sounded conversational, totally unlike his chilling rages. Almost disconnected from the swirling events. "They allowed the White House to send their blood hound Bannon sniffing around. And to make matters worse, they didn't even know until we told them." He pointed to the phone. "Let's hear what Ryker has to say."

Chloe unmuted her phone and said, "Peter is here with me.

Go ahead."

"Bannon and the sheriff met with hospital security for almost an hour," Ryker said. "Our contact with the security team wasn't present. We have no idea what they discussed."

"I've also heard from our contact inside the hospital." Chloe directed her words at Peter. Still coming to terms with this change in her mercurial boss. "The sheriff, his wife, and Eric Bannon are upstairs Lauren Crane's lab."

Ryker asked, "Who's your contact?"

"The microbiologist in charge of the lab next door." Aiming her words at Peter. "Last night our guy destroyed blood samples taken from the two recent cases that got away from us. Now the Washington agent and the Steens are in there."

Ryker gave the news a beat, then, "What about the doctor Jerry took from the rave?"

"Stacie Swann. She's still on lockdown in the county hospital."

"What do you want us to do?"

Chloe told her boss, "The number of people involved is growing exponentially."

"We could tail them when they leave, find a nice empty spot on the county highway," Ryker said. "My team is ready to roll."

Peter rose and walked to the window. And stood there. Unnaturally still for such a hyper guy. Finally, "Ryker, you and your team stay on Sheriff Steen and the agent. Surveillance only."

Ryker's impatience added a new rasp to that fractured voice. "It's time to do more than track and observe."

"Washington is watching, Chloe. Which means we have to be careful."

Chloe asked, "What about the two women, the nurse and the blood specialist?"

Peter nodded to the sunlit glass. "How many are left from Jerry's team?"

"Four, but they're not what you'd call totally reliable."

"Is one of them your top girl, what's her name?"

"Sybille's still on leave. The doctor said she's having muscle spasms where the agent struck her in the throat."

His only reaction to the news was to rock up on his toes. Down. Up again. Then, "So we've got the final four of Jerry's semi-losers, plus our guy who's still on duty in the hospital lab. Think that's enough?"

"For what, exactly?"

"Say we make a grab for the two ladies." His voice was beyond calm. He might as well have been describing a boat trekking down the St John's River. "Say our guys make the two women disappear."

Chloe rose to her feet. Crossed the room. Stood there beside him. As blind as he probably was to the world beyond their window. "Not harm them."

"Not unless it's necessary. Just make them…"

"Vanish."

Peter kept rocking. Up and down. "We don't say a word."

"No threats."

"Certainly not. If Bannon and the sheriff accuse us…"

"Which they probably will." Chloe began nodding in time to his movements. "We don't have any idea what they're talking about."

He glanced over. "You like it?"

"There's a high risk factor."

"That's something we've been living with for nine and a half months," Peter said. "Risk."

She studied her silhouette in the glass. A ghost of pale colors and electric fire. "Ryker, did you get that?"

"I say we should be the ones making the ladies vanish."

"It would leave the sheriff and the agent unmonitored," Chloe said. "We can't have that."

"You and your guys will be off the leash soon enough," Peter said.

Ryker asked, "Is that a promise?"

Peter's breath fogged the glass before his face. "You have my word."

Stacie used the hospital room's shower, then dressed in another set of hospital blues and entered the ER wing. She remained very unsettled by the episode. What she needed was work. Intense hours that forced herself to turn away from being chained to the bed and waiting for the drug's invasion. Her bloodwork was clean, she had slept enough to last a month, she was fine.

Only the lie did not take hold. No matter how often she repeated the words. She wasn't fine at all.

Just two cubicles were occupied. Dr. Henry was with one patient, the other was waiting for transfer to radiology. Stacie seated herself at the computer station in the ready room and pretended to go through case files for patients that had been seen while she was away. Only she could not focus. The words just swam. They might as well have been written in Arabic. She read and yet nothing registered.

Then it happened.

Her unsettled feeling coalesced into a flashing image. She knew she was still seated there in the empty room. She could hear the normal quiet chatter from the ER's reception desk. The main entrance sighed open, then shut. And in that instant, an unseen door opened inside her brain.

A new Stacie emerged.

The transition was all internal. She knew that at some instinctual level. No one saw anything amiss. Just the same...

She knew.

The words on the computer screen faded into a grey mist. In their place, Stacie glimpsed a mental image as real as any mirrored reflection.

She saw a beast.

The fiend wore her face. But the jaw was elongated, like a half human, half wolf. The normal human incisors were replaced by curved fangs that glistened in the electronic glow. The eyes were slanted, yellow, and very fierce.

She was involved in this internal transition, and yet she also remained the trained medical specialist.

The feeling was as exquisite as it was intense.

This was precisely the same transition she had witnessed in the female patient. Only now she witnessed the accompanying power and ferocity. A tidal wave of relentless force.

The most extreme sensation was one of freedom.

She was no longer Stacie Swann, the driven doctor whose lifelong ambitions had all been thwarted. In this singular moment, Stacie was offered the power to rip the bars apart and escape. Nothing could hold her.

The civilized veneer, the need for her superiors' approval, the constant yearning drive to advance...

Gone.

In its place was a wild intensity as potent as a forest beast.

She felt the power course through her veins, pushing her hands and feet into talons meant to grip and tear. Muscles that grew and rippled, ready to spring, to attack, to devour.

Then the beast before her eyes opened its mouth impossibly wide. And roared.

"Stacie?"

She jerked so hard she almost fell from the chair.

"I'm so sorry to have startled you." Dr. Henry stood in the doorway, watching her with concern. "Are you all right?"

"I..." She glanced down at her hands, the polished nails. She touched the smooth skin of her face. "I'm not sure."

"There's a new patient, I thought perhaps…"

"No, no, you take it." She turned off the computer and sat staring at her reflection in the dark glass.

Everything was normal.

It had all been an illusion.

Stacie reached for her purse and pulled out her phone.

It required four tries to code in Eric's number.

When he answered, she burst into tears.

Eric and Dewey were heading northeast on the two-lane 301 highway, passing through small towns still trapped in '50s-era poverty. They circled around lakes and orchards and pastures filled with narrow Florida cows. The heat was oppressive and refreshing at the same time. Dewey drove with the windows down and the A/C on high. The fragrances filling the car were a potent blend of agriculture and swamp mud and orange blossoms.

Then Stacie called.

Soon as Eric answered, Stacie's sobs resonated from his phone. Eric motioned for Dewey to roll up the windows so he could hear more clearly. Eric had never been particularly good at handling female emotions. Sitting in Dewey's car and watching the Florida wilderness sweep past, he flashed back to the rawest incidences with his late wife. When she had learned the family disease had struck her as well. When she had entered treatment. When this, when that. Eric's job had basically been to endure the sobs and the anger and try to offer comfort and strength. All the while he had felt utterly, completely helpless. Just like now.

Stacie needed a full three minutes to manage, "I never cry."

He struggled against his bitter inadequacy and said the only words that sounded right in his head. "If it had to happen, I'm glad I could be there for you."

She was silent for so long Eric figured she was trying to find a nice way to tell him his response was just so lame. Instead she asked, "Where are you?"

"About an hour northeast of Gainesville. Heading to Jacksonville. We can turn around."

"No, no." Stacie began crying again. "I'm so scared."

Eric was filled with the same hyper-awareness that had carried him through so many different stresses. Most of them had been in the field, of course. But not all. He knew the concentrated ability to parse the seconds, to hear the soft huffs of a strong woman rendered so weak she was incapable of drawing a full breath. He knew Dewey was casting him looks and appreciated the man's silence. He knew, he knew…

He knew all the regret he had felt standing over his wife's grave. All the unspoken things that had surrounded him. So many times he had been offered the chance to break free of his natural reserve.

He took a very hard breath and forced himself to wrench open the cage of his emotions. "When I first saw you in the ER lobby, I thought you were a living, breathing impossibility. Impossible that someone so beautiful could be so intelligent. So *aware*. A complete and utter professional. It would have been so easy for you to just coast. Accept that the male world wanted to offer you the bended knee."

Stacie huffed a few times, then managed, "It wouldn't have been easy at all. It would have been terrible."

"And you saw that. So you carved out a new definition of what this beautiful, brilliant, and passionately intense woman might become."

"Wait a minute." There was the sound of the phone being set down, then Stacie blew her nose. Again. She picked up the phone and asked, "How did you know what I needed to hear?"

"I didn't. I just knew I had to try." He paused, then asked, "Now will you give me the long version?"

* * *

Stacie's experience emerged in a series of tight snippets, short bursts of words and mostly unfinished sentences. It was utterly unlike the way she normally spoke. Her pauses were long gaps where she struggled to move beyond the pain of recollection and just *breathe*. Eric hoped the lady would not mind as he began relating the news to Dewey. But apparently the pattern of repetition actually helped her stabilize.

When she finished, she waited for him to pass on the final few words, then said, "Please tell me this is normal for trauma victims."

"You're the ER doctor."

"I know, but..." She huffed a few times. Then, "Up until that night at the rave, I only saw the aftereffects. Not the event itself. I suppose..."

Eric thought he knew what she was going to say. "You are the product of your profession. You are a highly successful doctor because you're able to remain detached. You analyze. You study. You decide how best to save a person's life. But it left you unprepared to be caught on the receiving end."

She breathed, "There you go again."

"What?"

"Never mind. Can this be trauma related?"

"It can happen. Battlefield survivors often endure flashbacks. Sometimes for years."

"But you don't think that's what I experienced, do you?"

Eric couldn't lie to her or offer false comfort. "You're not remembering something that happened. You have no direct personal experience to point you in this direction. So no. I think it's something else."

"Like what?"

He heard the fear and tension lift the tone of her voice. "It might still be trauma related, Stacie. The drug could also still be in your system. It could amp up your fears, make them seem real. We don't know what we're dealing with."

"What should I do? I don't want to go home. I want to stay busy, but I don't, I can't..."

"Maybe we should turn around and come back," Eric said.

Dewey said, "Tell her to call Carol. She's spent years soothing panic-stricken patients. She'll know what needs doing."

Eric passed on the suggestion, then waited.

Stacie's voice was little-girl small. "Will you do it?"

"Stacie, of course."

"It's just…I don't want to relive that episode again by telling it to someone else."

"I totally understand. You just hang tight. Either she or I will call you right back." But when he cut the connection, he just sat there, staring at the phone.

Dewey said, "You done good."

"I feel like everything I just said was only halfway there."

"Of course you do. It's part of being a guy trying to help a lady. Times like that, we define inadequate." Dewey tapped the steering wheel a few times, then said, "I was listening to you talk to her and thinking about Tyler."

"I know."

"If I ever find out who's behind this, I hope they enjoy their last few breaths."

Eric was thinking the same thing. "Give me Carol's number."

Stacie was still waiting for Eric to call back when the day nurse said a doctor was urgently needed in cubicle three. A child had come in with breathing difficulties.

Stacie talked her way through an extremely careful examination, starting with a search for an obstruction in the airway. It was doubtful the parents could hear everything she said, with the blue baby screaming through every wheezed breath. She listened to the chest and checked the little body for evidence. Then she found the red spot on the baby's left shin, surrounded by the pinkish rim. A clear indication of severe inflammation resulting from an insect bite.

The little girl was seven and a half months, and a real fighter. Stacie liked how the child watched Stacie's every action, willing her to stay focused, move beyond her own mysteries and make this crisis go away. Stacie sent the nurse to the pharmacy for a short-acting beta agonist, or SABA.

Ten seconds after injecting the dose, the baby stopped crying.

The child's response was a textbook case of how fast infants responded to proper treatment. Stacie wrote out an order for methylprednisolone therapy in case the symptoms returned and explained that the child would need to remain with them overnight for observation. She accepted the parents' tearful thanks, then excused herself and stepped into the corridor. And just stood there. Reveling in the sensation of having done her job, and done it well.

"Stacie?"

She was shocked to find Dr. Henry standing next to her. "I'm sorry, yes?"

"Are you all right?"

The concern was evident in his seamed features. "I'm not sure."

"You left your phone in the ready room. Carol called. She asks you to meet her at the university hospital as soon as you're able."

Stacie pulled into the Shards Hospital visitors' lot and sat staring at the front entrance. She had not been back since her firing. The administrators and lawyers all had different words for the way she was forced out. Polite and legal. But the truth was, she'd been dumped like yesterday's trash. Career shredded. Hopes demolished. Just another lonely lady wishing she could redo her mistakes.

Which was the problem, of course. She had done nothing wrong. Unless playing Don Quixote against the hospital's power structure with a broken lance had been declared a felony.

She slipped around the building and entered through the doors used by the cleaning staff. An electronic pass was required, but Stacie just waited until an employee exited. Someone who actually belonged.

The hall was scarred and ancient. This was the oldest part of the building. The corridor's clattering echoes whispered to her. All the dreams lost, all the regrets, all the futility.

She shared the staff elevator with two Latinas in yellow scrubs and an empty gurney. Stacie knew they had just delivered a body to the morgue. She considered it a suitably bitter welcome.

Carol and Lauren were waiting for her in the lab director's cramped little office. Carol greeted her with, "Eric called. I told Lauren what's happened. I hope that's okay."

The caring concern Stacie saw in both women's gazes brought

her close to losing control. "It's fine."

Lauren said, "Girl, I've missed you."

"I'm sorry I haven't been in touch."

"You got branded by El Comandante. You needed to put some space between you and the bad times." Lauren dismissed her absence with a fierce embrace. "You're doing what you need to. You're recovering. That's what matters."

"Stacie's doing a great job at county," Carol confirmed.

"Of course she is. It's the only kind of job my girl knows how to do." Lauren inspected her closely. "How are you?"

"Scared."

The two older women closed ranks, forming a barrier of caring concern between Stacie and the outside world. Carol said, "We're here for you."

"That we most certainly are." Lauren rolled over a lab stool. "Now sit yourself down. I'm going to draw blood, and you're going to give us the long version."

Recounting her experience in the doctor's station left Stacie feeling immensely better. There was no logic to the sentiment. Nor did she need any. She watched Lauren prepare her blood for examination and said, "I forgot just how cluttered this place was."

"How efficient." Lauren responded without looking up from her work. "How filled with brilliant people doing brilliant work."

Stacie looked through Lauren's office doorway to the waist-high glass partition separating them from the lab next door. "That's Palindrome?"

"Officially. Last week they temporarily shuttered their project."

"Any idea why?"

"Until today, my only concern was getting my lab space back." She set the vials into the centrifuge and started it spinning. "That used to be the other half of my department."

Carol said, "I remember you complaining about that."

"Loudly and all the way to the board. Not that it did me any good." Lauren's phone chimed. She pulled it from her pocket, checked the screen, and handed it to Carol. "It's his secretary. You know what to say." As Carol slipped into the lab, Lauren continued to Stacie, "You're not the only one that Benny has burned."

Stacie watched as a weird little guy emerged from the other lab's office. "Who's your pal?"

"Gary. Extremely strange, but apparently harmless." She halted the centrifuge, waited for it to stop spinning, and opened the top. "They had a dozen or so people working in there. Then overnight they vanished. Everyone but Gary." Lauren opened the top. "Say the word, I'm happy to arrange an introduction."

Gary resembled a lot of aging lab geeks Stacie had known. Scraggly hair dangled from a large central bald spot. Shapeless face the color of old dough. Black square spectacles. Belly straining against the stained lab coat. "Tempting. But I'll pass."

Carol stepped back inside and told Lauren, "It's all arranged. El Comandante will see you in fifteen minutes."

"Who did you say you were?"

"Your new lab assistant."

"Perfect." Lauren said to Stacie, "You're coming."

"No. Definitely not."

"Girl, I was not asking."

Carol offered Stacie a huge smile. "This could be fun."

"Nothing about seeing that man again could be defined as fun."

"He thinks Lauren is coming up to discuss a potential new discovery her lab has made." Carol's grin was almost wicked. "Which is true, if you consider Palindrome's lab to be still hers."

Lauren said, "Tell me you won't enjoy watching Benny squirm."

Carol said, "I for one wouldn't miss this for the world. I've only met him once and I already despise him."

Lauren halted Stacie's next protest with a flat palm. "I've got a syringe filled with happy juice, and it's got your name on it. You can come high or you can come straight. But, girl, you are coming."

Chloe told her boss, "I really think you should let me handle this meeting on my own."

"And my response is the same as the three other times you brought it up." Peter lifted the file he was reading. "Less than four pages? Really? This is all they could put together on Eric Bannon?"

"It's not bad, for a covert operative. There's more on the sheriff."

"Forget Steen. He's a ride-along. Bannon is our target."

"Which is why I should be in there alone. Deniability could be crucial in a situation such as this."

"Your warnings are becoming monotonous." He flapped the file shut and tossed it onto her desk. "I'm involved and I'm staying. Deal with it."

Asking Peter to bend was a risky endeavor. Like most of the 412 employees of Palindrome's headquarters, Chloe generally avoided it. When Peter exploded, there was always fallout. But this was different. She genuinely did not think it was wise for him to be seen by these investigators as personally involved. But that was not why she kept at it. She had already resigned herself to the inevitable.

Chloe kept talking because she was trying to feel her way through totally new terrain. She felt as though the two of them had entered into a new phase. Something was at work that she did not recognize. Despite the current disagreement, she felt as though she and her boss were...

In sync.

Like two top operatives in a live-fire, high-risk environment. Her life depended on trusting the other guy. Knowing at a level beyond thought or advance planning that he would do what was necessary, back her every move, and not leave the field of battle without her.

She said, "Okay."

"Okay what?"

"I accept that you're participating. That your input is important. And I will back your play."

She could have expected him to blister her over that comment. Pretending that the decision was hers when the boss was seated on the desk's other side. But all he said was, "Good. That's good."

She wanted it out there in the open. "Because we're a team."

He eased deeper into the chair. Peter rarely sat anywhere. He perched. Like a bird of prey hunting his next target. But he was relaxed now. "That's right, Chloe. We are."

"Will you tell me why you feel this is so important?"

"Because you're thinking in the past tense."

"Explain."

"You're still on damage control. We're way beyond that. Our entire construct is blown. This isn't about three missing pens, or a lone wolf agent whose file has been totally redacted."

She was reading him now. And something more. Chloe experienced a sudden coalescing of energies. "Eric Bannon's presence threatens to take us all down."

"That is correct."

"He could wreck our dream. I thought we were airtight," Chloe said. "I was wrong."

"You can't take this on your shoulders," Peter said. "I won't have you falling on your sword."

"I designed our cover as a series of concentric shields. This is my—"

"Correction," Peter said. "*We* designed it. And I approved every step. The problem is not your construct. We were assured by our Washington allies that we were safe from federal scrutiny. They told us to proceed. We trusted them to keep us safe. We designed a protocol that would have been solid, if they had done their job. They failed us."

Chloe studied her boss, trying to read behind the words. "You've had a word with our Pentagon contacts."

"Oh no. You're wrong. Why waste time with those jokers? I went to their bosses. Actually, I went three stages higher. By close of business today, the guys who failed us will be reduced to three dark stains on the Pentagon's parking lot."

Chloe leaned back. "Will you tell me what they said?"

"Of course. We're a team, aren't we? They said, meet the enemy and report back ASAP. From the sound of things, they're standing by the phone. This has become highest priority with some very powerful figures."

She nodded slowly. Digesting the fact that they were now part of a much larger series of events. And risks.

If the White House power structure gained enough intel to officially declare this an issue, there was every chance these generals would wash their hands of the entire affair. Eliminate her, Peter, their team. Erase them as swiftly as possible.

People so close to the throne had no time for prisoners. The last thing top DOD decision makers wanted was somebody with damaging intel lurking in the shadows. It was far easier and safer to simply delete the risk.

Chloe said, "Our only hope lies in dealing with the threat."

"Right."

"Which is why you're sitting here."

"Right again." Peter's ease had a name now. He was fully committed. "I expect we'll soon have an opportunity to see just how bad Ryker and his team can be."

* * *

Ninety minutes later, Eric and Dewey threaded their way through Jacksonville's terrible traffic and crossed the downtown bridge. The city held far more in common with Atlanta and Savannah than the rest of its own state. The median age was twenty-six, the energy vibrant. Palindrome occupied an enviable spot overlooking the Saint Johns River and the city's skyline. Eric assumed the architects had designed the steel-and-glass headquarters to suit the ego of the guy signing the check. The building suggested a place with no room for sentiment, no concern for the people occupying the vast marble-clad lobby. They were merely players. They came, they worked, they sweated, they gave their all, and they were forgotten even before they slipped back out the sliding glass doors.

As soon as the woman emerged from the elevators, Eric knew she had come for them. All of one piece, was how Eric's first mentor would have described her. As tightly structured as a sniper's weapon, and far more deadly. Her pale blond hair was waxed into a tight helmet. Her outfit was sleek, understated, and fit her like the silver filigree on a high-end hunting rifle.

The sheriff's phone chose that moment to ring. Dewey checked the readout and said, "It's Tyler."

Eric turned his back to the approaching woman. "Take her photo when you're done."

"Hold on a second, Tyler." Dewey lowered the phone a trifle. "Say again."

"This woman could be our key," Eric said, talking swiftly now. "Forward it to Tyler, see if he knows her. Send it to me. I'll have the ambassador check her out."

Eric turned back and walked toward the woman, putting distance between them and the sheriff. "Are you looking for me?"

"That depends." She stopped only because Eric blocked her path. "You are?"

"Eric Bannon. I assume somebody's alerted you to our arrival."

Her gaze was a green laser. Not emerald, nothing so refined. More of a military green, the color of two gun barrels in the sunlight. "Why is that man taking my picture?"

"I think you know."

She gave that a beat. "Are you armed?"

"No. But obviously the sheriff is."

"You will need to relinquish all weapons and electronic devices. No exceptions."

"Roger that." Eric started to turn away, then asked, "Does that include your company's pen?"

Eric and the woman stood just outside the entry as Dewey locked his weapon and both their phones in his vehicle. The woman was not a talker, at least, not to him. She did not speak again until the two men rejoined her. She spun around and said, "Follow me."

Dewey asked, "Isn't this the point when the lady introduces herself?"

Eric replied for the silent woman, "Her name doesn't matter."

Dewey followed them back inside. "Why do I feel like I'm tracking slower than everybody else?"

Eric stayed quiet while the woman obtained two visitor badges and ushered them through the security turnstile. When they stared at their reflection in the elevator doors and the woman still had not responded, he said, "Every branch of the military has its own brand of intelligence operative. Army, Marines, and Navy mostly rely on their special forces for covert actions. They develop a certain way of functioning in enemy terrain."

Dewey demanded, "Is that where we are now?"

Eric chose to ignore the question. "The separation between covert and analysis is huge. Communication goes up to the top, then back down again. Which is both good and bad."

Two young staffers pushed through the turnstile behind them and headed their way. The woman shot them a glance. Not more than two seconds. The staffers backpedaled away.

Eric went on, "The Air Force always did things differently.

Most of their intel budget goes to eyes and ears in the sky. Their operative side is small, elite, and very impressive. Each field agent is a manager. This sets them apart. They will work as a team, but they are also trained to think and act independently. Analyze, decide, strike."

The elevator pinged and the doors opened. Dewey waited until they were inside to ask, "You worked with them?"

"Twice."

"Does the lady here know about that?"

"Doubtful. Both actions were intended to stay permanently under the radar. My file was probably redacted."

The woman spoke for the first time. "Three and a half pages. That's all we got."

Eric went on, "Having a former Air Force covert operative meet us says a great deal. Military suppliers have a revolving-door policy toward retired officers. One hand washes the other. But Palindrome's official remit is supplying the VA hospital system."

"Having this lady on staff says different."

"More than that," Eric said. "Her presence says they're not hiding the fact. Why should they? Since they know we know."

The doors pinged open. Three people waiting for the elevator lost their smiles and stepped well back. The woman gave no sign she saw them at all.

She led them down the side of a vast bullpen and opened the door to a glass-fronted conference room. She ushered them inside, shut the door, and walked away.

"Scary," Dewey said.

"You have no idea," Eric replied.

"I need to tell you—"

"Not here," Eric said. "They're monitoring our every word."

Stacie reluctantly followed Lauren and Carol along the admin corridor and into the hospital director's office. Benny Benitez's secretary was a legend among the hospital staff. Mona had dark hair and a flat seamless face. She wore only black, shoes to hair clip. She guarded Benny's office with a possessive sullenness. Lauren put on a smile as fake as the veneer covering Mona's office walls. "My, but don't you look a picture today? Is our dear leader available?"

"Don't call him that."

"You know I didn't mean any disrespect, Mona. Why, there's nobody on the hospital staff who thinks more of dear Benny than me."

"He's Dr. Benitez to you."

"Well, of course he is." Lauren offered the same impish smile she had shown Stacie. "Shall we just waltz on in?"

"He's busy." Mona eyed Stacie as she would a spoiled sample of alien tissue. "Dr. Benitez didn't say anything about her."

"Oh, but Dr. Swann is crucial to the topic we're here to discuss. Isn't that right?"

Carol cheerfully agreed, "Absolutely vital."

"And you are?"

"I'm sorry, didn't I mention that already? Carol Steen is a senior ER nurse at the county hospital and wife of the sheriff. She's here in an official capacity. Isn't that right, dear?"

"Doesn't get any more official than this," Carol agreed.

The ladies' banter and Mona's irate responses faded into a vague background murmur. Stacie found herself once again caught in the duality of experiences. She was acutely aware of her surroundings, but viewed everything from a vast distance. She was also helpless to do more than observe as all her tension and sorrow and past regrets fed on the place and the hour, growing larger and denser, until it became...

Something else.

The rage burned in her now. An impossible fury that was both hers and utterly alien.

Mona's phone rang, and reluctantly, the secretary allowed them to pass. Carol and Lauren maintained their cheerful banter, thanking the secretary profusely and wishing her a really, really nice day. Really. Stacie heard it all, her vision remained crystal clear, and yet a veil existed between her and the outside world, one electrified by this latent fury. Just waiting for an excuse to expand and take control.

Benny Benitez's office was larger than Lauren's entire lab. Stacie had been here once before, when she had confronted the hospital director over the incident. She had expected him to apologize. Ask for another chance. Dredge up some excuse or another. Instead, he had merely smiled. The prince of his domain, safely ensconced on his throne, eyeing her with utter contempt.

He was not smiling now.

"What is that woman doing here?"

"Her name is Dr. Swann," Carol said.

"I know her name. I asked you..." Benny shrank back into his oversized executive chair as Stacie closed the distance.

Which was very odd.

She knew she moved because she could observe the change in her perspective. One moment she stood by the door. The next she hovered over his desk. Like she had flown there. Swept down on predator's wings, talons at the ready. There for the kill.

"Hello, Benny."

"Don't call me that!"

"I'll call you whatever I like." Stacie could not fathom why she had ever been frightened of this plump, oily little man. "How is your girlfriend? Oh. Hang on. She's not your girlfriend anymore, is she? You dumped her. She's...Wait, it will come to me. Hasn't she relocated to Miami? Amazing how a trainee nurse could land a senior post at the university hospital. And without even an interview. Do I detect your hand at work, Benny?"

"Get out of here!" Benny found something so appalling in Stacie's presence that he could not take his eyes off her as he scrambled for the phone.

Stacie leaned in closer. The rage had control now. She felt it boiling through her, a surging tide that left her...

Invulnerable.

She heard herself say, "Put down the phone, Benny."

But inwardly, where it really counted most, she heard something else.

Stacie snarled.

The sound rippled through her. Like a current. Electric and deadly.

Benny Benitez froze.

"Now then," Stacie said. "You and I are going to have a little chat."

"I didn't mean the young lady any harm!"

"Forget the girl you molested, Benny. She is ancient history. You've probably had several others since then. No, we want to talk with you about..."

Lauren said, "Palindrome."

"Right. Your pals at the company who drugged and abducted me."

"I...What?"

"They kidnapped me, Benny. They dosed me with a chemical they had designed for military intelligence. Designed right here. In the lab you arranged for them to steal. From Lauren. But I escaped. And now I'm here. So you can tell me what you're doing, covering up their mess."

"I don't know what you're talking about!"

The internal force continued to build. Stacie had a sudden awareness of the sheer *potential*. If she allowed it to truly manifest, if she released the power fully, she would...

Change.

And if she did so, if she allowed herself to make the transition, there was no coming back.

The realization came to her from the level of bone and sinew. She had no need for analytical logic. She could feel herself standing on the verge. And it was so very tempting. The thrill of giving into the vicious undercurrent was almost overwhelming.

But the professional side of Stacie's makeup saved her. The years of struggle and study and discipline and analysis proved stronger still. She took a mental step back and whispered, "No."

"Palindrome is just one of a hundred investors in this place! I haven't had contact with them in weeks! All I know is, they halted their lab work! I assumed it was a cut in funding, but I can't even say that for certain!"

Stacie felt a shudder run through her, an immense outflow of energy and rage. She took another step away from the desk. In so doing, her perspective of Benny Benitez underwent a drastic change. He was no longer prey, there to be consumed. He became once more merely an ego-driven, sweaty little man.

Stacie heard the tremor of release in her voice. But from the terrified look Benny gave her, he mistook it for fury. "These women have some questions. You will answer them, Benny. You will tell them everything they want to know. Or I'll come back. And you know what happens if I do that, don't you?"

The hospital director actually squeaked, "No. Please."

"One more thing. Palindrome is to be kicked out of the lab. Lauren gets the room back. And all the equipment. Today." When he did not speak, Stacie said, "Let me hear you say it, Benny."

"Yes, of course, I'll…"

"Good. Very good." Stacie turned around and saw the two women watching her with twin round-eyed expressions. She observed how they shrank away from her as she passed. But there was nothing she could do about that now. "He's all yours."

At first glance, Peter Sandling appeared the polar opposite to the lady who followed him down the outside hallway. The blond woman was a military operative dressed by Versace. Peter Sandling was a billionaire in a crew-neck sweater and round tortoise-shell glasses and leather high-top sneakers and black skinny jeans. He bounced to some internal tune as he talked with two employees outside their conference room. The woman was still as glacial ice. A grey-suited older woman maintained a deferential position three steps behind Peter. The staffers were almost slavish in their gratitude for whatever their boss signed off on.

He waved the pair off, pushed through the glass portal, waited for the grey-suited woman to follow him inside, and demanded, "Who's on point?"

The blond woman said, "Eric Bannon is consultant to Ambassador Reeves."

"I know that name."

"Theodore Reeves is former head of State Department intel, currently serving as White House advisor on issues related to national security."

"Of course. I met him, right?"

The grey-suited woman nervously flicked through files on her electronic tablet. "I have no record—"

"Never mind." The guy twisted in his seat like an impatient kid. "What are we doing here, Agent Bannon?"

Eric took his time settling into a seat that had not been offered. He jerked his chin at Dewey, who had remained standing by the side windows. Only when the sheriff had selected a chair did Eric turn back. Communicating that this nervous CEO was not in control. No matter how many operatives he had inside his checkbook. "I think you know."

Parchment streaks extending from his eyes and mouth made a lie of his smile. "Enlighten me, Agent Bannon."

"Tell me about the weapons you make."

The guy's only response was to jerk his chair back and forth, back and forth, the human metronome unable to keep proper time.

Eric went on, "We're specifically interested in the pens designed for defense intel. The ones that don't show up on any VA manifest."

Sandling flicked imaginary lint from his sleeve. "Not much I can tell you, Agent Bannon."

"But you make the weapon pens."

"We did. Not anymore. Not for…How long has it been?"

The grey lady replied, "Three years, two months, and twelve days."

Eric asked, "What was the drug you inserted in those weapons?"

"This is where the lawyers get involved." He waved to the grey lady standing by the glass wall. "Tell them, Agnes."

The attorney was scarcely taller than Peter Sandling was when seated. She had a mask for a face and a voice that matched her outfit. "Agent Bannon, our remit specifically—"

"It is Mister Bannon," Eric replied. "I've been a civilian for seven years and counting. I assume that you as their legal advisor would be interested in getting things right."

"Our remit specifically forbids discussion of this and all related topics." She opened a leather portfolio and drew out a clutch of stapled pages. "The related paragraphs are highlighted."

"For your reading pleasure," Sandling said. "Are we done?"

"We'll need to arrange another appointment once these orders have been overturned," Eric said.

"Tell your boss the Joint Chiefs eagerly await his call." Sandling waved his hand. "Give him that too."

Agnes passed over a single sheet. "This is our designated contact with the JCS."

"Can you tell me if you were the only group to manufacture these weapons?"

Sandling nodded, as though approving the question. "The only group we know of."

The blond spoke for the first time. "Careful, boss."

"I'm well within their parameters. The answer to your question, Agent Bannon, is, we have no idea. DOD gave us the standard remit. Design, test, report, cost, build. If there was another group, we never heard directly about them. But the military thrives on rivalries. If one doesn't exist, they'll create it."

"So you're saying…"

"Too much," the blond said.

"Every time we got behind schedule, they threatened us with how another group was chomping at the bit. How this other group had promised to supply bigger, faster, better, cheaper."

Eric said, "You asked around."

"Of course I did. Wouldn't you?"

"Absolutely," Eric said. "I'd hire an Air Force covert ops who knows how to hunt in hostile terrain and remain utterly unseen. I'd issue orders to track down the rumors. And I'd give her everything she asked for."

The blond woman said, "Time to wrap this up."

Sandling told Eric, "We found nothing. Nada. So to answer your question, we assume we're the only suppliers. Or rather, we were."

Eric knew why they were still sitting there. He had known it ever since the guy showed up. But there was nothing to be gained from rushing things.

He waited.

Sandling finally asked, "You brought a pen with you?"

"No," Eric replied. "But I did bring one of the recovered weapons."

Sandling went still for the first time. "Let me see it."

"I'm happy to discuss the possibility," Eric replied. "In time."

Sandling's rage compressed his features further. This was definitely a man not accustomed to having terms dictated to him.

The attorney said, "At this point I feel obliged to—"

"Get out," Sandling said. "Now."

The grey-suited woman tossed Eric a furious glance and departed.

Eric lifted his gaze to the blond woman standing behind her boss. "And you are?"

Sandling didn't like the tables being turned. But it was either respond or leave. "Chloe Pernil, my head of security."

"You look tired, Ms. Pernil. Why don't you have a seat?"

At a nod from her boss, she walked over to the table's opposite side and took the chair next to Dewey.

Eric said, "Three questions."

"One," Sandling snapped. "Ask."

"Tell me why the drug is considered top secret," Eric said. "Three years after it went off-line."

Sandling leaned back. Took his time inspecting Eric. Finally he said, "I think you know."

"I can guess."

"Boss!"

"Either get with the program or get out," Sandling said. He kept his gaze on Eric. When Chloe remained silent, he went on, "I'll answer your question. Will you show me the pen?"

"Sure thing," Eric said. And pulled the evidence bag from his pocket.

Chloe Pernil rose from her chair and walked back around to stand beside Peter. She leaned in tightly but did not place her hands on the table. Nor did she handle the plastic bag containing Eric's pen. She left no trace of her passage. Typical.

Peter lifted the bag, drew it close, and asked, "Did you bring the glass?"

Chloe slipped a magnifying glass from her pocket and handed it over. "There's no tag."

Dewey spoke for the first time since the corporate executives had entered. "Tag?"

Eric said, "Every military item is required to have a traceable ID tag. It can be letters, or a number, or bar code, or all of the above."

Sandling asked, "Can we keep this?"

"That was not part of the bargain."

"My lab could give you some solid intel on the drug."

"Sorry. No. That article is now property of Ambassador Reeves." Eric held out his hand. "Maybe your contact at JCS should give him a call."

Reluctantly Sandling returned the item. "To answer your question, the design was stolen. We have no concrete evidence of who was behind the theft."

"We know," Chloe said. "There is absolutely no doubt whatsoever."

"We *suspect* one of our on-staff bio techies."

"It was Kevin," Chloe declared. "It had to be. He's the only employee who's left since the counterfeits started showing up. And we can't find him."

"Kevin Lassiter," Sandling said. "A real piece of work."

Eric found himself filtering their words through a hard-earned internal lie detector. What he had left was…

Smoke.

Their words drifted into the background. He heard himself speak when they invited, listened as Dewey offered a few comments of his own. But mostly he examined the pair seated across from him.

They were as tightly matched as hand-crafted dueling pistols. They spoke and acted and lied as one unit.

Eric had met people like Peter Sandling before. Beneath the

preppy clothes and the mercurial personality that clearly terrified his employees, Eric suspected there lurked a chameleon. A man who could lie with every breath, because at that moment he actually believed what he said. An actor who lived and worked on the stage of his own making. Always in the spotlight. Living for the chance to spin his next myth.

Chloe was something else entirely, a carefully honed assassin in Versace silks.

Sandling drew the room back into focus by telling his aide, "Go call our guy with the Joint Chiefs. Ask them for formal permission to discuss. Tell them the cat's already out of the bag."

"There's no way they're going to accept that news, coming from me," Chloe replied.

"No, you're probably right." Sandling rose from his seat. "This shouldn't take long. But since it's the Pentagon, there's no way to say for certain. If you need something, use the phone on the side table."

Soon as they departed, Dewey pulled a pad and pen from his shirt pocket, wrote hastily, then asked, "How long are they gonna keep us sitting here?"

"If we're lucky, not long at all."

He slipped the pad back into his pocket, but as he did so he tilted it so Eric could read what he'd written.

We need to talk NOW.

Dewey said, "Ball park."

"They probably kept us waiting earlier so they could report in. If the Pentagon brass are as worried as Sandling indicates, somebody is poised by the phone, waiting for their report."

"You think I've got time to check in with my duty officer?"

"Probably." Eric was already up and moving. "Let's take it outside. I want to alert the ambassador."

"What are they doing now?"

Chloe stood in Peter's office, by the window overlooking the parking lot. "They're both working their phones. The guard at our front desk heard Bannon ask for Ambassador Reeves as they exited the building."

"Can we listen in?"

"The sheriff's phone should be hacked and accessed soon. There's no telling with Bannon. His phone was not acquired under his own name. And he hasn't called us, so we have no way to ID his device."

Peter was busy signing a pile of legal documents that had been deposited on the center of his desk. He frowned as he worked. "Can we target their conversations?"

"They're standing under the trees lining the visitor's parking area. We'd have to get a parabolic mike at ground level."

"Bannon warned the sheriff the room was miked."

"Of course he did. Don't jump to conclusions."

Peter hesitated and glanced over. "So…you think they bought it?"

"Hard to say." Chloe continued to survey the sunlit lot. "You did good back there."

"You think?"

"You made him fight for every inch." Chloe smiled at the

glass. "It was a class act."

Peter signed the last document and pushed them away. "I want to call in Ryker's team."

Chloe had been expecting this. "If you're absolutely certain."

"We've got our DOD allies pushing hard as they can for this entire mess to be dropped. We take Bannon out, it's unlikely in the extreme that Reeves will manage to send anybody else."

"And the sheriff?"

"You already know the answer to that. We use the pen, insert a new memory. He's had an accident. Hit and run. Bannon didn't make it."

"You know the memory swipes leave scars."

"So Steen suffers a concussion. He never fully recovers." Peter rose from his chair and walked over to stand beside her. "It happens."

Chloe pointed with her chin at the pair emerging from the trees. "Here they come."

"Call Ryker. Have him ready his team. And get somebody down there to wire the sheriff's ride for sound." Peter watched the two men enter the main doors. "Tell Ryker once they leave the building, he needs to give the pair time to call in their reports. Then he's to erase them both. Only leave the local lawman still breathing."

Stacie took the stairs from the admin floor down to the lobby. The last thing she wanted was to be alone. Being out there in her car would only make things worse. So she headed for the main cafeteria.

She greeted two staffers she recognized. But she did not pause and they did not press her. The university hospital complex employed over eleven hundred personnel. Stacie would still be known by many as just another resident, a face they saw repeatedly in the normal course of a frantic workday. For many of the non-medical staff, Benny Benitez was despised as a Napoleonic tyrant. Stacie had not ever realized the depth of loathing that man instilled in the general staff until her own troubles started. Then slowly, quietly, one person after another came up and confided in her. How they wished someone would just make him go away. How they admired her for what she had tried to do. How they would miss her. How they wished they had her nerve.

Stacie bought a tea and fruit salad, then found a quiet corner by the rear glass atrium wall. A pillar and a stone trough holding shrubbery formed a mock wall. The hospital cafeteria offered a remarkable blend of privacy and public space. She tried to reach Eric, but his phone went straight to voice mail. Stacie sipped her tea and replayed the incident in Benny's office.

The fear over removing the lid from her internal cauldron was no longer present. She had retreated from the edge. She had resisted the furious urge to leap over the precipice. Stacie had no idea what might have happened if she had given into the urge. But just then it mattered less than the fact that she had maintained control.

Then the man who had kidnapped her at the rave entered the cafeteria.

Eric got on his phone while he and Dewey were moving through the main reception area. When his boss answered, Eric asked to be put through to the ambassador. He spoke loud enough for his request to be overheard by the guard manning the reception desk. He pretended to listen, then said the ambassador needed to return his call ASAP, because Eric urgently needed to file a verbal report.

When they exited the building, Eric selected a tree fronting the parking area. He spoke softly, a murmur, nothing more. "Stand here in the shade. It'll mask us from any rooftop listener." When Dewey joined him, Eric said, "Plant the phone to your ear, but turn it around so you can cover the microphone with your hand."

"They've hacked my phone?"

"Probably not yet. But we need to assume it's going to happen. This is for the watchers."

"What about your phone?"

"Mine came with the job. It's not a registered number, so unless I call them directly, they don't know which number to track. What did you want to tell me?"

"The call I took before we went inside."

Eric used both hands to cradle his phone and pretended to tap the surface with his thumbs. Just shooting off a couple of emails. "Tyler called you, right?"

"It wasn't from Tyler. It was from a woman." Dewey

pretended to cut the connection, then scrolled down his screen. "Just shows her number as private."

"The woman who called, did she have a name?"

"Probably. But she didn't offer it. She asked if you were around. When I confirmed, she said to tell you she was your dance partner at the rave. And that she is the only reason why Tyler is still alive."

The instant Stacie spotted the attacker from the rave, she ducked down and pretended to fumble in her purse. But all the while she watched the man and relived the incident. That confrontation marked the second time her life had been effectively stripped from her control. First Benny, then by this man who now walked around the hospital cafeteria. Acting like he owned the place. Like he belonged.

She had only seen him for a few moments while he had smiled and waited while two other men had grabbed her from behind. Then he had reached out and touched her neck. And gradually everything had faded away. The next thing she'd known was Eric calling her name.

She could almost hear Eric now. Telling her to be strong. Stay alert. *Focus.*

Even viewing him from across the room, Stacie knew it was the same man. He was tall and solidly built, with what she had always considered a boxer's neck. The trapeziums and the sternocleidomastoid muscle groups were so overdeveloped they formed a triangular slope from his jaw to his shoulders. He wore a black-knit T-shirt just like he had that night. Shaved head. Diamond earring. And he moved like a dancer. Slipping quickly around the room, scouting.

She remained crouched beneath the table as his gaze passed over her. Then he turned and left the room.

Stacie had to assume he was also looking for Carol and Lauren. It all made sense. Her mind hunted at a frantic pace. So the attacker had come in search of three women…Why now? As soon as she shaped the question, she had the answer.

She and Carol were asking questions. Closing in on everything the people behind her attackers wanted to keep hidden.

So now he was back.

Stacie felt the resurgence of rage and power. There was no way his strength could take her down a second time. Not if she gave into the lure. It was stronger now than in Benny's office. Her friends were being threatened. Her *friends*.

It was so very tempting to let go and release the power and see how much havoc she could wreak.

Chloe emerged from the building and invited Eric and Dewey to return upstairs. Peter Sandling was there waiting for them in the conference room. Eric sat and pretended to listen as the CEO and his hired gun continued to paint a pretty picture. All the while, he focused on peeling away Sandling's carefully burnished mask. Taking aim.

Thirty minutes later, Eric followed Dewey out of the building and over to the sheriff's vehicle. Neither man spoke until they settled into the cruiser. Dewey shut his door and said, "I've got about a dozen questions."

"That makes two of us," Eric said. Pulling the phone from his trouser pocket required some adjustments, as the passenger side was doubly constricted. A pump-action shotgun was held by a locked metal frame that pushed against his left shoulder. And the sheriff's computer was in another frame that jammed his knee. "But first I need a couple of minutes to digest what we've learned."

"What about—"

"Hold that thought." Eric typed swiftly, then held the phone up for Dewey to see. His message read, *Don't speak a word about Tyler. Or our destination. Call your dispatcher, check in as usual, and say we are headed back.*

"Let's go," Eric said.

***

Stacie remained crouched behind her table after the kidnapper's departure, trying to reach Lauren or Carol on their phones. Both went straight to voice mail. Stacie texted them a pair of tense warnings, then stood, checked the surroundings one final time, and raced for the nearest stairwell.

She flew down the long corridor connecting the majority of the hospital's treatment centers to the ER wing.

She arrived in the middle of the late-afternoon lull. She forced herself to a walking pace past the main reception desk and down the side corridor. When she arrived at the pharmacy, two patients stood before the narrow window. Stacie hovered just out of sight, trying not to dance in place. When the patients departed, Stacie stepped forward and tapped on the pharmacy door's glass partition. Three seconds later, the woman she'd hoped to see opened the door and said, "Stacie?"

"Juana, hi. Can you let me in please?"

Soon as the pharmacist unlocked the door, she slipped inside. She endured a three-second embrace, then said, "I have a problem. It's serious."

Stacie had heard the rumors so often she had to assume they were true. How the Latinas on staff got it the worst from the hospital director. Which was strange, given that Benny was Cuban. But the macho attitude was fiercest in the face of upstart Latinas who used the American culture to rise up, to excel.

Juana must have seen something in Stacie's expression because the words seemed to form from the fear in her gaze. "Is it Benny?"

"Sort of. Maybe. I'm not actually sure...I have three men out there who are hunting me. They're employed by a group that's financed the lab next to Lauren's. They kidnapped me."

"Oh, that's terrible! When?"

"Three days ago. I escaped. Carol Steen, you know her?"

"The name, yes."

"She's a nurse at county. ER. Her husband is the sheriff—"

"Of course I know of her. I hear very good things."

"She's upstairs. I think she and Lauren are in terrible danger."

Juana had come to know Stacie as one of the few residents who treated the pharmacy as anything more than a drug dispensary. Stacie had prowled the aisles, demanding to know everything she could about the drugs on offer, their doses and side effects and possible alternate uses, what to do with children, how they affected male and female patients differently, their impact when used in conjunction with other pharmaceuticals. In the process, she and Juana had become friends and allies both. The hospital's chief pharmacist demanded, "What do you need?"

"A cocktail that will send them into next week."

"I have just the thing." Dark eyes sparked with a malicious gleam that Stacie had never seen before. "Use the pad there, write me up a prescription for Ertapenem, Oxaprozin, and Diazepam. But it won't send them to next week, my dear."

"No?"

Her hands were already busy. "I am thinking more like, some distant galaxy far, far away. How many doses do you need?"

Peter stepped back into Chloe's office and demanded, "Anything?"

"Close the door." When the glass portal sighed shut, she said, "Sheriff Steen called his headquarters and spent twelve minutes discussing standard police-type trivia. He said they were headed back. Bannon got a call back from Ambassador Reeves and gave him chapter and verse."

"Bannon didn't deviate from what we fed them?"

"Not an inch."

Chloe watched as her boss slipped the phone from his pocket, stepped to the far corner, and spoke too softly for her to hear. Three minutes later he returned to the visitor's chair and started his bounce routine. The man actually looked pleased. Excited, even.

Peter Sandling said, "It's time to let Ryker and his team take them out." When Chloe did not respond immediately, he went on, "If we're ten seconds too late, word gets out. Now we have an option for a clean break."

Chloe took careful stock. It was something from her frontline days. Marking the transition from surveillance to action with a gut-check. While there was still time.

Peter went on, "I've had a word with our allies in the Pentagon."

"And?"

"They concur. Bannon has given the ambassador our chapter and verse. That is now the official line, just as high up the food chain as it can get. And something else. Bannon is going to keep hunting. Sooner or later he's going to come up with evidence that contradicts our version of events."

She nodded, not so much in agreement as acknowledging the time had come. She studied her boss, wondering how he would hold up with the bullets started flying.

Peter met her gaze. Steady. Determined. As if he knew what she was thinking. "Talk to me."

She said the first thing that came to mind. "I seriously doubt we will ever describe an attack by Ryker and his team as clean."

"Be specific in your orders. He does it our way, according to our rules." Sandling bounded from the chair. "Are we clear?"

"Yes, we're clear. But I don't know if Ryker will actually follow—"

He headed for the door. "Chloe, you've got your orders. I've got mine. Tell Ryker he's to do precisely what is required."

Juana insisted that Stacie bring in the security duty officer. Trey listened to Juana's rapid-fire summary for less than ninety seconds. "Dewey and his pal from Washington, what's his name?"

"Eric Bannon."

"Right. They already gave me the long version. Lauren's in danger because of this mess with the new street drug?"

"She might be." Stacie hesitated, then added, "Actually, I'm ninety percent certain."

"Then let's move out." He lifted the radio from his belt. "I want to call in two of my staff."

Juana grabbed his arm. "Did you just hear what she said? We don't have time for you to bring your peeps up to speed."

"My peeps. That's a good one."

Stacie saw the way they looked at each other, and realized Trey and Juana were a couple. She said, "Every second counts."

"Listen to the doctor," Juana said. "We are not wasting any more time, not with my friends in danger."

"They're my friends too. And this is security. And the number-one rule in situations involving a threat is, never go in alone."

"What you mean, alone?" Juana looked genuinely incensed. "Do I look like a stuffed piñata to you?"

"You look like a lovely lady who needs to step back, is what."

"You big handsome macho *idiota*." Juana swiped his arm.

"Go back to watching your monitors, why don't you?"

"Too late. And no hitting the security, else I may need to cuff you."

Stacie said, "All I need is a diversion. Give me a chance to get in close."

Trey looked from one lady to the other. He must have seen something in their gazes, because he replied, "I ain't saying yes, mind. But I'm listening."

Stacie assumed that was as close to affirmative as the man was capable of coming. She ran through what she had in mind, then finished with, "Trey, if they try to touch you with a pen, run."

"Girl, they're the only ones running anywhere today."

She was already moving. "We need to hurry."

Stacie spotted them the instant she emerged from the stairwell. Trey had timed it perfectly, arriving via the elevator a few seconds before them. He approached from the corridor's opposite end, moving down t-he hallway toward Lauren's lab. The two men and a hard-faced women stood looking through the window in the door. Stacie could not recall the others. Not that it mattered. The woman tapped on the door and pointed to the door handle. Stacie knew the only reason why her friends were still breathing was the electronic lock.

Her friends.

Stacie hung back as Juana started down the hall, then followed with her face pointed at the floor. They were both dressed in surgical blues, right down to the cloth booties, and carried instrument trays. As unthreatening as they could make themselves. The trio glanced their way, then turned back to Trey.

The rage lurked just below the surface of Stacie's calm. The lure to engorge herself on the power, consume the temptation and grow into whatever prowled on the other side of that electric veil. Stacie had never considered herself a brave person. But there was no room for fear now, not even facing three kidnappers in a hospital corridor.

Trey bopped his way down the hall. "Say, hey there. Can I help you folks?"

The brute who had fronted Stacie in the warehouse separated himself from the others. "We have business with the lab director."

"That so. You got an ID?"

"This is a public establishment." The man revealed a subtle accent, one he clearly tried hard to disguise. "No ID is required."

"Actually, friend, that is totally not correct. The hospital is private. Visitors are welcome only so long as I say. And I'm saying to you, show me some ID."

"Of course, Officer. No problem." He gestured to his mates, then reached behind him. "I have it right here."

Stacie was moving before the hand came back around holding the pen. She gripped one of the syringes and took aim at the closest assailant, which happened to be the woman. Stacie jammed the needle into her left shoulder and hit the plunger. The woman shrieked, reached back, and slumped.

The second man was much faster than Stacie had expected. He spun and violently blocked Juana's syringe.

Stacie did the only thing that came to mind, which was throw her remaining three syringes at the man's eyes. When he lifted his arm to block, she slammed the metal tray into his face. He roared and came at her, which granted Juana both time and space to jab him with her needle.

Stacie scrambled on the floor for one of the unused syringes, then came up searching for the third attacker. But the man was already prone on the corridor floor, still jerking from the impact of Trey's Taser. Juana took a fresh syringe from Stacie and jammed it into his leg. The security chief rewound his cables, surveyed the two who were moaning softly, and asked, "You recognize any of them?"

"The one by your feet was my kidnapper."

Trey leaned over and started cuffing the trio with zip-ties. "In that case, you're all under arrest."

The only thing that saved them were Lauren and Carol yelling from inside the lab.

Stacie spun and faced a monster.

The supposedly harmless creep of a lab geek pushed through his own door and launched at them. He moved with astonishing speed. The door leading to his own lab was still closing, slow as a lazy summer afternoon, and he was already on Juana. He was larger now, his frame so engorged he had shredded the lab coat. The material hampered his movements, such that he kept trying to shrug it off, instead of mauling the screaming pharmacist.

Trey slammed the Taser into the back of his neck and fired.

The creep spasmed backwards, shrieking at the ceiling. But he did not release Juana.

It was then that Stacie realized she still held a syringe. She jammed it into the point where his neck met the angle of his jaw. In the soft spot just behind where the bone curved was a cavity in the durra matter known as Meckel's cave. This natural hollow contained the semilunar ganglion, the point at which all the sensory nerves of the trigeminal system joined together.

The geek might have been made super strong and he might have felt invulnerable. But the ganglion was a biological pain center for all the nerves in the head and neck.

When she plunged the needle home, the shock was so violent the man froze solid. Every muscle in his body locked.

Stacie pressed the plunger and stepped back. Leaving the needle exactly where it was.

The marauder gave a manic shriek, then the drugs took hold.

The three of them in the corridor, and the two women gaping through the glass partition, watched as the giant slumped to the floor...

And melted.

Three frantic breaths later, Stacie looked down at just an unconscious overweight geek in a mangled lab coat.

But what she really saw was what she had managed to avoid. The next step along the dark path. What would happen if she gave into that rage.

The beast she now carried inside herself.

The security lock buzzed. Lauren opened the door and Carol

demanded, "What on earth?"

"Everything is fine," Trey said. He bent over and started fastening plastic cuffs on the four. "I'm telling you, the doc here is totally stand-up."

Dewey drove them another forty-five minutes along the I-10 corridor, gradually leaving the city traffic behind. When the first rest stop came into view, Eric pointed. Dewey responded by saying, "You mind if we pull in here a second?"

"No problem."

Nothing more was said until they parked and left the car. As they walked toward the building, Dewey asked, "They bugged the car?"

"If I'm right about something, absolutely."

"And if you're wrong?"

"We're doing a song and dance for no audience."

"I got no problem with being overly cautious. That's why you talked to your boss like you did?"

"Different song, same audience."

"Your boss knows that?"

"The Ambassador is the ultimate professional."

They used the facilities, then walked over to the man-sized state map at the center of the shaded central area. Dewey asked, "So you don't buy what they told us?"

"Tempting. But no."

"Will you tell me why?"

"Gut, mostly. But a couple of things just don't mesh. Now I want you to run through what the lady caller told you about

Tyler. Don't leave anything out."

"She gave me a grand total of ninety seconds. She asked for you. I said first she needed to tell me why. She claimed to have Tyler, then she mentioned that you two met at the rave."

"She had Tyler? As in, she'd kidnapped him?"

"I asked her that very same thing. The lady replied that she was the only reason Tyler was still breathing."

"Anything else?"

"She gave me a number. Said for you to call."

"How did she sound?"

"Scared. Maybe a little hoarse. She kept coughing."

"I chopped her in the throat."

Dewey grinned. "You got some way with the ladies."

"This is Eric Bannon. Is your phone secure?"

"It's a new pay-as-you-go, bought with a fake ID. This call's come in by way of a satellite-internet feed." The woman sounded exactly like Eric thought she would. Tough, military direct, slightly hoarse. "How do I know it's really you?"

"I'm switching to video feed now." He hit the button, directed the camera at his face, said, "Remember me?"

"Yes. Now it's my turn."

"Wait. I want you to swing in a slow circle, give me a clear view of your surroundings."

"This is no trap, mister secret agent."

"Show me."

She did as he directed. Eric drew Dewey over so they could both watch. Eric saw a riverside shanty on tall stilts with a rowboat and aluminum motorboat tied at the end of a derelict pier. There was nobody else, nor any natural cover. Just the shack. Eric saw a lumpish shadow flitter into shape beneath the house, heard the clink of chains. He assumed it was a guard dog, possibly a wolfhound. He asked Dewey, "You recognize anything?"

"Absolutely," he replied. "I know about a thousand places

just like it."

The woman demanded, "Who's with you?"

"Sheriff Steen. What's your name?"

"Sybille. Sybille Atkins."

"You told the sheriff you have his nephew."

"I want a guarantee of full federal immunity. I've got the goods. But only when I know I'm shielded from prosecution."

"And in exchange you'll release Tyler Brock?"

"What *release*? There is no *release*. You still don't get it at all."

"So tell me what I'm missing."

"I'll do better than that, Agent Bannon. Watch carefully, now."

Eric and Dewey stood shoulder to shoulder as the view bounced in time to her footsteps over the rough terrain. She shifted away from the stairs leading up to the shack, circling into shadows. When the camera adjusted to the dimmer light, Eric and Dewey gasped in unison.

The shanty's foundations were thick as telephone poles and darkened from the creosote used to treat them against rot. The black surface of every stilt was scarred with long claw marks, some deep enough for the timber to leak frozen amber tears.

"Come on out, sweetheart," Sybille said. "It's time for your close-up."

The chain clinked once, twice. Then a beast sprang at them. The speed was so incredible Eric jerked away from the phone. He fumbled and only barely managed to keep it from falling to the concrete.

The beast was definitely a female. And probably once had been human. Now she was...

Something else entirely.

She howled at them with unbridled fury.

Sybille cut the video feed but kept the audio link. They listened as she soothed the beast, calming her down to the sort of hoarse grunts a lioness might make.

They listened as she stepped away, then demanded, "You still there?"

"I'm here."

"Full immunity," Sybille repeated. "Call when it's in place and I'll give you coordinates."

Twenty minutes after they left the interstate and reentered the Florida countryside, Stacie called.

Within seconds of hearing her first semi-gasped words, Eric cut the connection and turned off his phone. He told Dewey, "I need to stop."

"Should be a place up ahead a ways—"

"Dewey, I need to stop *now*." Just as the car pulled onto the verge, Dewey's phone rang. Eric plucked it from the center console and turned it off as well. He opened his door, and said, "Must have been something I ate."

Eric led Dewey to a stand of stumpy pine and wild palm. He stood well back in the shadows and watched the road. When he was certain they were not being tracked he said, "Something's gone down at the medical center." But when Dewey reached for his phone, Eric said, "Hold on a second."

"I want to check on Carol."

"I know you do. Stacie says they're okay." Eric handed him the phone. "We need to decide something first. Do we still meet with the woman and check on your nephew?"

Dewey stared at him for a long moment, then hit the speed dial. Eric moved three steps away and called Stacie. She answered with, "I lost you."

"I had to make sure we weren't overhead. Tell me what's

happened." Eric listened to her breathless description, then said, "You handled that like a pro."

"I can't believe you do this for a living."

"I'm retired, remember? Where are your assailants?"

"Cuffed to gurneys and totally zoned out on Juana's special cocktail. Hospital security is swarming. The police are due any minute. They want us to go to the station."

"Let me check with Dewey." He waited for the sheriff to disengage from his wife. "Tell me what you want them to do."

"Carol assures me they're okay. They're surrounded by hospital security. Gainesville police are inbound."

"Do you have allies on the Gainesville force?"

"Dozens," Dewey replied. "More."

"Have them keep the whole group under tight wraps until we get there. Not a word to anybody."

"They'll do that, if I ask them."

"Then let's go find Tyler."

Dewey made a couple more calls, then returned to the vehicle and made a big thing of insisting what Eric needed right then was a dose of deep-fried Florida country cuisine. He overrode Eric's mock protests and drove them further and further into swamp country. Their destination lay down a one-lane road that sparkled white-silver in the afternoon sun. Dewey rode with all his windows down and the A/C on high. "What you see here is a relic of the Florida I knew as a kid. A lot of our early roads were paved with crushed oyster shells."

Their destination was a place called Catfish Junction. Eric thought the restaurant lived up to its name. The rough-plank walls and ceiling framed a scene from bygone days. The floor was unvarnished wood, the tables covered with sheets of unbleached paper. The restaurant was ringed by diners enjoying their meal on blankets along the sandy riverfront. The parking lot was full of pickups with gun racks and fishing gear and canoes. The food was outstanding. Both men ate with the determined appetite of experienced troopers.

Twenty minutes later, Dewey pointed a pair of greasy fingers at a Dodge truck backing an airboat toward the boat ramp. "That's our ride."

Eric watched the narrow man settle his airboat into the still waters, then lash it to the dock. "What kind of motor is that?"

"Airboat jockeys use just about any old thing, long as it's loud and fast. I believe he lifted that off a Shelby that lost a late-night quarrel."

"So it's fast."

Dewey grinned. "You never been on an airboat before?"

"Never even seen one up close."

"You know those pictures of astronauts going through training, their faces get all squished back by them fancy speed machines? NASA should've brought their trainees down here, taken them out on an airboat, saved the taxpayer a billion dollars."

The airboat skipper climbed into a tall chair set high above the two padded rows in the bows. The name painted in Day-Glo orange down the boat's side was *Gatorbait*. He fiddled with the controls, pushing his rudders to one side and then the other. Eric asked, "You trust him to get us where we're going?"

"There ain't no road signs on the Saint Johns," Dewey replied. "Only hope we have of finding this place is if that old boy takes us."

Chloe said, "Start from the beginning."

Ryker's voice was the same dry rasp as always. He spoke in a cadence one step off bored. "They ate a late lunch at a riverside joint. They strolled down to the dock. The sheriff stopped several times to talk with people. Then he made a call."

"Hold one." Chloe linked her computer to the monitoring software her inhouse teckie had finally managed to insert into the sheriff's phone. "All right. What time was that?"

"Fifteen, twenty minutes ago."

She read off the screen, "The first call we show after we got this up and running was at three eighteen. Steen phoned his office." She clicked on that entry and the sheriff's languid voice filled her office. She asked Ryker, "Can you hear?"

"Loud and clear."

Dewey asked his dispatcher, "We got anything cooking back there?"

"Sheriff, it appears that the whole county has gone quiet."

"That's what I like to hear. Where are my duty officers?"

The dispatcher ran through a series of positionings, mostly traffic watch and paperwork, one vehicle on prisoner transport. Chloe thought her tone was hesitant, like she was uncertain how to take the absence of any crisis. Dewey responded with, "Carol got held up by some altercation at the hospital, nothing serious by the sound of things. If she calls, tell her I'm taking our big-city friend on a little ride, show him Florida's hidden side."

"Sorry, Sheriff, I don't—"

"I won't be reachable for a while. Tell my wife I'll check with her when we get back in range."

Chloe cut the connection, then said to the phone, "What happened next?"

"He and the Washington agent talked to one of those airboat jokers. You know what I'm talking about?"

"I've seen pictures."

"They took off, I called you. End of story."

"Can you follow them?"

"Not without alerting a whole restaurant full of hicks to the fact that we're tracking a local lawman. And even then, it's doubtful. That airboat started up and blasted away. The Saint Johns is not your normal river. It meanders through the lowlands in about a thousand different directions."

Chloe tried to draw up the sheriff's location, but he and his phone were clearly out of cell range. "Stay in position, alert me the instant they return."

"Roger that. Ryker out."

Soon as she cut the connection, she relayed the conversation to Peter. Her boss shrugged and demanded, "Steen's taken his new DC pal on a boat ride. We wait and take them out when they return."

Chloe could give no name to the electric nerve-worms crawling around her gut. In the end she remained silent.

"What happened at the hospital?"

"I have no idea. None of our crew is answering." She sighed. "I hate being cut off like this worse than a firefight."

"What, you think our four guys couldn't handle three women?"

"I can't say for certain. I couldn't even say how that might have happened. But I'm worried."

Peter made two circuits of her office before responding. "I

talked with Washington again. Their response was two words: damage control." He was as grim as Chloe had ever seen. "Tell Ryker, soon as that pair return, he is to go in fast and hard. Soon as that's done, he has to find the women."

"Maybe I should join them."

"No, I need you to direct things from here." He reached for the door, then added, "Make sure Ryker understands, we don't have room for any more loose ends."

The airboat's noise was a constant trio of roars. The motor was a five-liter V-8 whose exhaust manifolds were less than two feet long and had no baffles whatsoever. The fan-blades were seven feet in diameter and bellowed almost as loud as the engine. And then there was the wind.

They all wore airfield-style goggles and headsets which reduced the clamor somewhat but rendered any conversation impossible. The wind was a constant force. It battered Eric's entire body. But strangely, he did not find it uncomfortable. He sweated, but the wind dried his perspiration as fast as it formed.

Their pilot was a taciturn man who had been reduced to his rawest elements by heat and humidity and lifestyle. His eyes were the clearest blue Eric had ever seen. It was a gaze intended for vistas without any hint of civilization, as clear and guileless as a hawk's.

After their meal, Dewey had walked Eric down to the end of the pier, pausing now and then to greet folks. Eric had spent the time studying the collection of airboats lining the beach. The contraptions looked impossibly fragile to hold the sort of power latched to their sterns. The flatboats were aluminum or steel, between sixteen and thirty feet long. They all held rows of choir-style seats across the front. Some of the cushions were hand-stitched with designs that suggested a rawboned sense of humor. The families who picnicked along the shoreline suited their rides. They were sun-blasted and heavy-set and quietly cheerful. When Dewey arrived at the pier's end, their pilot had already fired the engine. Dewey shouted an introduction as he climbed on board. The pilot's name was Hank or Harry or Heck or any number of possibilities. He gave Eric ten seconds of a rock-hard grip, spat over the rail, released the boat's two lines, climbed into his perch, and blasted away.

Their velocity was immense. They skimmed over the surface so fast the foliage along both banks formed greenish-brown pastel blurs. Eric estimated they were traveling at somewhere around seventy miles an hour, but it could just as easily have been a hundred. If they struck a log or a gator, he doubted the exact speed would be all that important. A low-flying bird might well bullet straight through his head. But there was nothing he could do about either, so he repressed his standard desire for ironclad control and gave into the sheer unbridled joy of...

Speed.

The shack was a small, elevated cabin, maybe thirty feet square, with a broad porch extending out over the water. At a signal from Dewey, their pilot cut the motor. They drifted about fifty feet off the pier's end. Dewey unclipped his holster guard and studied the terrain. Finally he said, "Looks calm enough."

"The brush is cut well back," Eric agreed. The stilts rose from a clearing that extended a good 150 feet from the riverbank. Beyond that, the foliage formed an impenetrable wall. "It would be tough to pull off an ambush."

"Ambush ain't the problem out here," the pilot said. "It's hogs."

"Excuse me?"

"Wild pigs. Domesticated animals gone loose."

"Snakes too," Dewey added. "And gators."

"It's mostly them hogs you got to watch out for. They's nasty beasts. Only animals in this country that'll attack a man outta pure meanness." The pilot spat over the gunnel. "You think my boat's fast, you wait 'til you see a hog come blasting outta the brush. Out here, you clear it back far enough to give you time to spot, unholster, aim, and fire."

Dewey said, "Which means these folks are down-home savvy."

The pilot asked, "You don't know who lives here?"

"They called, we answered," Dewey said.

"Most of these folks ain't partial to outsiders." The pilot pulled a twelve-gauge from a holster attached to the side of his chair. He cocked both triggers and said, "If they ain't in a welcoming mood, I sure hope they go for you first."

Eric asked, "How far to the nearest road?"

"Ten miles, maybe more," Dewey replied.

"Don't mean nothing," the pilot said. "Only way in or out is by water. You wouldn't make it half a mile in this brush, city boy."

Eric kept his eyes on the shadows beneath the house. "I don't see the beast. But it looks like the chain is lying there in the dirt."

Dewey said, "I wouldn't like to set foot out there if that thing is unleashed."

"Smart move," the pilot said. "Most of these outliers, they keep some nasty guard dogs."

Then the woman stepped out of the home's shadows. Sybille walked to the porch railing, put her hands on her hips, and called down, "You plan on sitting out there until dark?"

Dewey demanded, "Where's the thing we saw?"

She turned around. "Don't worry, mister law man. I've got everything under control. For now."

The pier was bowed and warped. The ground between the dock and the shanty was carpeted with weeds and stumps and fist-sized succulents. The steps were nailed into the side of the house and trembled under Eric's steps. Dewey saw him hesitate and said, "This cabin is built from live oak. It'll be standing long after a grandaddy hurricane blows the rest of Florida to Louisiana."

Eric checked the terrain a final time. The low rumble of a gas-powered generator emerged from a shed further along the shoreline. The cabin's support poles were all scarred with claw marks. But the beast was gone.

He followed Dewey up the steps. Three voices sounded from inside the shanty, two female and one male. But Eric sensed nothing that indicated an imminent threat. The three people were just talking.

Dewey said, "Look down there behind us."

"I see it." The chain lay strewn across the ground leading back to the foliage. At its end was a complicated sort of padded leather harness. Empty.

Dewey stepped onto the porch and stayed well back from the doorway. "Tyler, you in there?"

"Thanks for coming, Uncle Dewey."

"Why don't you join us out here?" When the cabin remained silent, Dewey added, "There's nobody out here except me and

Eric. We've already seen what happens."

The woman Eric had decked in the warehouse stepped back into view. "You want to understand, you come inside. Don't worry, you're perfectly safe."

The parlor's four windows were covered by old-fashioned wooden slat shutters. Blades of afternoon light cut the cabin's occupants into tight segments. Eric disliked the lack of clarity. But he sensed no danger.

Dewey, on the other hand, was growing madder by the minute. "Tyler, I warned you back on that very first day—"

"And you were right. And I should have listened." The young man sounded beyond exhausted. Utterly spent. Defeated. Resigned to his fate. "But I didn't. It might have been too late then anyway."

"It was," Sybille said. "Way past quitting time."

Sybille had taken position against the wall by the left window. Tyler was a shadow huddled on the floor to the right of a mangy sofa, his back against the rear wall. The woman Eric had last seen snarling into the phone's screen was curled up on the sofa. Despite the languid heat, she had a blanket pulled up to her chin. At least Eric was fairly certain it was the same person.

Dewey remained standing with his back to the door, one step inside the front room. His right hand rested on the pistol's grip. "What have you gotten yourself into?"

"Dewey," Eric said. "Settle."

"I want some answers here!"

"We all do." Eric gripped the sheriff's arm, pried the hand loose from his weapon, walked him over, and seated him at the kitchen table. He pulled out a second chair and positioned himself close enough to halt Dewey if he tried to rise. "That's what we're here for. To get answers." He asked Sybille, "All right if I make a call?"

"There's no signal out here. You got to hook up through an internet dialing system. We've got Wi-Fi through a satellite dish."

Sybille pointed to the phone lying on the kitchen cabinet. "Be easiest just to use mine."

Ambassador Reeves had insisted on being part of this initial debriefing. He wanted to personally give Sybille her green light. Eric understood the man's reasoning. The ambassador wanted immediate bonding and total access directly with the source. Timing was crucial because as soon as DOD found out, there would be a mad rush to raise roadblocks. Reeves needed direct contact. He wanted to be there for the receipt of the raw intel. No interpretation. No terse abbreviation.

Plus, Reeves knew there was a very real risk Eric would not survive.

Eric rose from the table and retrieved the woman's phone. The sheriff merely kept glaring at his nephew. The young woman on the sofa moaned softly and rolled over, or tried to. Sybille squatted down and stroked the girl's cheek, speaking in a voice too low to catch. Eric thought her tone was surprisingly gentle for such a hard-edged assailant.

Dewey's question came out as a bear-like rumble. "What's the matter with her?"

"Withdrawals, mostly." It was Tyler who responded. "And exhaustion. So tired you can sleep a million years and still wake up shattered. Every bone in her body, every joint, aches like it's on fire. She'll have a low-grade fever for another couple of hours."

"Tyler..."

"You wanted answers, Uncle Dewey. That's what I'm trying to offer."

Eric coded in the ambassador's private line. When Reeves answered, Eric asked, "Can you hear me?"

"Five by five."

"I'm here with Sybille Atkins and two test subjects in recovery mode. Our host is the woman who was part of the warehouse attack group. We are safe. She has offered to supply what we need to know."

"Do you trust her to deliver?"

For Eric, there was no longer any question. "She already has."

"All right. Let's do this."

Eric rose from the table, walked over, and handed the woman her phone. "Ambassador Reeves is former head of State Department Intelligence. He now serves as White House advisor on intelligence."

Sybille did not take the phone. "How do I know this is legit?"

Reeves heard her question, for when Eric raised the phone, the ambassador said, "Tell her to call back through the White House operator. She needs to get the number from information to believe it's real. I'll alert them to pass through the incoming call."

But when Eric passed on the instructions, Sybille said, "Never mind. Give me the phone." She rose to her feet and said, "This is Atkins."

She listened for a time, then simply said, "Copy." She handed Eric the phone and said, "Let's get started."

Eric set the phone on the table, hit the loudspeaker button, and asked, "Ambassador, can you hear us?"

"Loud and clear."

Eric crossed the room and lowered himself to the floor beside Tyler. "Will you tell us what's going on?"

"Sybille should do it." Tyler gestured to the woman squatting by the sofa. "She can give you the big picture. All I can talk about is what it's like on the inside."

Eric asked, "And how is that?"

Tyler lifted his head. He looked straight at his uncle for the first time. "There ain't no way to tell or even imagine how great this is. Every limit, every weakness, it's just gone."

The young woman on the sofa pushed herself up to a sitting position. She tucked the blanket up around her chin and said, "Or how awful it is once it's over."

"There is that," Tyler said.

"The guilt is..."

"Suffocating," Tyler said. "Hard as death."

Dewey shuddered and started to speak, then glanced at the phone resting by his elbow and stayed silent.

Eric studied the young man. The room seemed frozen in the amber of shadows and slatted light. "So it's great and it's dreadful."

"In equal measure," Tyler said. "But once the bad hour passes..."

"The bad half day," the young woman corrected.

"The hunger to do it again is..."

"Awful," the young woman said. "Awful, awful, awfully good."

Eric asked, "So you have the ability to make it happen when you want?"

"When you *want*," Dewey muttered.

"Not always," Tyler replied. "But yeah. We can bring on the change. It gets easier with time."

"Smoother too," the woman said.

"And faster," Tyler said. "Real fast, if need be. Like, an explosion you can almost hear."

The young woman said, "The longer we hold back, the stronger the need to bring it out again."

"The *need*," Eric repeated. "The need to do *what?*"

"There's only one way you'll ever understand," Tyler said.

The young man shifted slightly away from Eric. His muscles rippled as he moved. Suddenly Tyler's features went from the supple strength of a young man into...something else. His jaw and forehead both extended slightly. His teeth...

They *grew*.

The tips of his ears rose into a narrow point. The fingers laced around his knee lengthened and from them extended...

Claws.

Tyler did not breathe now. He grunted.

Eric had heard that sound before. The last year that his wife had been in full health, they had taken a photograph safari together into the Kenya high savanna. One night a lion had crossed through their camp. The slight cough that punched each breath was that of a marauder in killing mode. Just like now.

Eric asked softly, "Can you control this power?"

Tyler huffed through three breaths, or coughs, or growls. He gave no sign that he heard Eric at all.

"That's not the question," Sybille said, still stroking the young woman's cheek. "You're totally missing the point."

"Explain it to me," Eric said, forcing himself to stay calm.

"You don't release rage or lust or whatever it is that raises your heart rate to redline," Sybille said, "and then want to stop and talk about *control*."

Tyler rumbled softly, deep in his chest. His eyes were golden now, the pupils slits of a brilliant yellow fire.

"You *are* this power," Sybille said. "A funnel for the force."

Tyler lowered one hand to the raw-plank floor and drew four claw marks in the wood. His unblinking gaze did not waver. He remained intensely focused on his uncle.

Eric tasted the air between them. His gut said this newly rendered beast was not a threat. At least, not in this very instant. But all professionals knew an animal born to hunt could never be fully tamed. It was a moment-to-moment thing. One day, without warning, an event would launch the beast into full attack mode. It could be nothing more than a wolf's howl on the moonlit wind. Or even the scent of grilling meat. Once that happened…

The fangs and claws and strength and speed and raw savagery were all there for a purpose.

"What you're seeing is the purest form of this power." Sybille had not even glanced at Tyler. "Once the transformation happens, there is no separation between the force and the individual. Everything about the person and the situation has just become redefined. Starting with that word you used. *Control*."

Tyler did not rise to his feet. He uncoiled.

Eric rose with him. He wanted to stay at eye level with this… This beast.

Tyler was a good foot taller now than Eric. His muscles stretched the cloth of his T-shirt and shorts until they looked spray-painted. He exuded an aura of unbridled menace. The parlor's air vibrated with his force. His feet clenched the floor as he arched his back, opened his mouth—and *roared*.

Neither Sybille nor the younger woman gave any sign they had even heard. Eric, however, felt the power resonate at the level of bone and sinew. His heart pounded, his muscles jerked and spasmed from the effort required to remain as he was, weaponless and stationary. Within claw reach of this...

Beast.

Sybille turned and looked at the sheriff. Dewey was frozen in place, watching his nephew with a rounded, tragic gaze. Sybille said, "Speak his name, then tell him to settle."

Dewey remained locked on the sight of his transformed nephew.

Sybille raised her voice. "Sheriff, listen to me."

When he did not respond, Eric said sharply, "Dewey."

The sheriff jerked slightly. "I...What?"

Sybille repeated her instructions. When Dewey hesitated, Eric asked, "Why say those words, and why him?"

"Because Tyler has bonded with him."

"Bonded," Eric said.

"The sheriff is the only one who can control him." She snapped her fingers in the air between them. "Come on, Dewey, wake up. Say the words, let him come down. Then I'll explain."

An hour and eighteen minutes later, Peter reentered her office and demanded, "Anything?"

Chloe had been pacing the room's confines, stretching the fabric of her too-tight skirt with every stride. Her office had never felt so constricting. She stalked back to her desk, hit speed dial, and turned on the phone's speaker. When Ryker answered, she barked, "Report."

"Same as twenty minutes ago. No sign of our guys."

"You have a clear line of sight on the car, the restaurant, the pier?"

"The works. The sheriff's ride is parked nose-out by the restaurant's front door. We're across the road from the parking lot entrance and three trees back. The sun's behind us. We're invisible and can scope out everything."

"Call me the very second they show."

"Copy that."

She cut the connection and resumed pacing.

Peter watched her for ninety seconds, then said, "Obviously you're locked onto a worst-case scenario that completely escapes me."

"You sure you want to hear?"

"Hey. You've already made me totally nervous. I might as well know why."

"Say that Bannon guy didn't buy your song and dance. Say his report to Washington was all a ruse. He's sharp enough to know we might have inserted a listening device into the sheriff's ride. Say he was making his own version of a play."

"To what end?"

"Sybille hasn't called in. She's not officially listed as MIA because I haven't posted it yet. And I still can't raise any of Jerry's remaining team."

"You checked with the safe house?"

"There, the lab, the online docket where they're supposed to register their movements. Sybille has vanished." Chloe made another circuit, then gave voice to her fears. "What if she and the agent are meeting? Right now. Somewhere along the river, where we can't monitor them."

Peter settled himself on the interior glass wall, his back to the bullpen. "But Bannon was the guy who took her out. He's the last person on earth she'd want to hook up with."

"Here's where my worst-case gets really bad."

"Go on."

"What if Sybille decided it's all falling apart? We still have the two chrysalis unaccounted for. Say Sybille gets hold of one or both of them. Tyler is the sheriff's nephew, remember. Sort of, anyway."

Peter snapped his fingers. "And that missing girl..."

"Kathy Palmer. Right. No relation to Sybille, but they go way back. Say Sybille gets hold of Bannon through Tyler and the local lawman, and she offers them a trade. Details of our tactics and methods, in return for full immunity."

Peter shook his head. "That's a stretch."

"I know."

"But terrifying."

"As bad as it gets. It would destroy us."

"So...what? We close up shop?"

"If this is going down, absolutely."

"On the basis of a bad afternoon? That's absurd."

"It's more than that." Chloe resisted the urge to shout and wave her arms. She had never hated her glass cage more than now. "Sybille is *missing*. The chrysalis are *missing*."

"All right. All right." But Peter was clearly not all that concerned. "You're forgetting one thing."

"I'm not forgetting anything."

"Ryker has been looking for a chance to show his potential. And our Pentagon bosses..."

"Would love to see what happens when you unleash him against real assailants," Chloe finished for him.

"So Bannon and the sheriff come back with the three of them. Ryker is right there. How much chance to you give them against our players?" Peter actually smiled. "Ryker and his guys won't even leave the bones."

For Sybille, it had all come down to money.

After basic training, she had shunted straight into Air Force Intelligence. There she had met Chloe Harper on her final assignment. Who had offered her a gig with more money attached than Sybille had ever dreamed of. Which had brought her here. To a shanty on stilts at the boundary of nowhere. Talking to the silent White House listener by way of a satellite dish. Trying to find her way out of a mess that was partly of her own making.

For most of her seven years in the military machine, Sybille had been tasked with supplying AF special forces with real-time data. The typical AF geeks tended to prefer duty in dark, warehouse-type operations, where they sat for their entire tour, watching the world through eyes in the sky. Satellite and drone operations consumed most of the AF intel budget and every noncom who showed the required abilities.

Sybille had served with a much smaller division. She and her fellow agents had been directly involved in frontline action.

In the past, military special forces had a love-hate relationship with most intel and DOD operatives. There was considerably more hate than love. The saying among AF special forces was, the most dangerous thing on earth was an officer reading fresh intel.

Special forces needed this intel, but most of what they received was worse than garbage. AF special forces called it flack. It was confusing. Hesitant. Vague. Out of date. Written to protect the intel division chief, rather than help the guys in Indian country.

Eric knew most of this, but left Sybille to complete her wind-up at her own pace. She explained how the Air Force began inserting an intel officer into every special ops team going up-country. The result was a complete and utter transformation of the intel sent to frontline troops. Data was distilled, reports were streamlined, intel became focused on target and task and extraction. Troop losses plummeted. Good agents became as vital to the team's survival as medics.

As a result, intel officers with frontline experience changed. They began viewing intel as another weapon. They learned what every soldier knew instinctively. It all came down to protecting their brothers and sisters in the field. When the guns blazed and the sky darkened and their next breath was uncertain, everything else became secondary.

This new breed of agent wanted to see intel become something more.

They began asking questions among themselves. They were tightly linked now, these intel officers who were also battlefield survivors. What else could they do to help their brethren? What could possibly turn the tide in their favor? Say there were no limits, not to budget nor to what they could accomplish. What would they most like to see happen?

"A report was prepared and passed up the line," Eric said. He felt as though he could read the script there on Sybille's features. "The concept had huge potential."

"And it arrives just as they make contact with this company in Jacksonville. Huge research labs. Big presence already in the VA hospitals. They set up a plan, and they start moving forward. And everything goes great. Until the problem arises."

"A big one," Eric said. Moving in sync with her now.

"Huge," Sybille agreed.

"Once their subjects make the transition, they can't be

controlled."

"Actually, they can, but only if they bond to the person who will serve as their one and only boss."

Eric pointed to where Tyler was curled up on the floor beneath the side window. He was just Tyler again. Sort of. He lay on his side, breathing in little gasps. Knees up midway to his chest, arms tucked around his legs. Watching them with a gaze that flickered in the slatted light. Eric asked, "He answers to one voice. And the voice isn't the guy they put in charge."

Sybille nodded slowly. "That's it in a nutshell. The crisis point. The reason it all fell apart."

"He *answers*," Dewey half-yelled. "Do you even *hear* yourself?"

"Yes," Eric said. "I do."

Sybille said, "Tyler knew it was going to be his uncle soon as he entered the chrysalis phase. In this respect, he's similar to my girl here. Bad home life, but they move forward anyway because of someone they rely on. Who cares for them. Someone they've trusted since day one."

Eric looked down at the young man. "You knew when this chrysalis phase started?"

"Right after the third dose. A little earlier than most users."

"Which is how he got away, same as my girl," Sybille said. "They don't start monitoring users until dose five."

Tyler panted a few breaths, then added, "Looking back, I think I knew what was coming from that very first taste."

"There is no such thing as a warrior gene," Sybille said. "But there are a lot of identifiable traits that go into making a warrior. And many of them are located in and around the brain's pleasure centers. Go after one, you intensify the other."

"Simple," Eric said.

Sybille shook her head. "Anything but."

The young woman's name was Kathy Palmer. She had risen up now and sat on the sofa with her knees tucked under her chin and her arms wrapped around her calves. The blanket covered all but her face. Sybille showed an astonishing gentle side, even in the smile she cast at the young woman seated beside her. "Kathy is the daughter of a friend who didn't make it back from Afghanistan. Kathy's had her share of problems." Sybille sat so one hand could stroke the young woman's neck. "Most of them started with drugs and good-time guys. Isn't that right, darling?"

Dewey checked his watch. Eric understood. The light was a butter yellow now, a gentle warning that daylight was waning. Eric said, "Two things I don't understand."

"Just two?" Dewey muttered.

Eric asked, "Who runs this operation?"

Sybille nodded. "That's a very good question."

"And the answer is…"

"Chloe, the woman who recruited me, handles the teams. Very tight chain of command."

"And the teams are run by…"

"His name is Ryker."

"Ryker is many things," Kathy murmured. "All of them scary."

"How many in Ryker's teams?"

"Last I heard, there were six plus the man himself. Human trials started five months back. Roulette is only made available through raves."

"Word is, the military considers drug users to already be willing volunteers," Kathy said.

"Five doses or more before the transition starts," Sybille continued. "Only those who bond to Ryker are allowed to survive."

Eric's next question was interrupted by a shout from the river. Dewey rose and walked to the open doorway. He waved down, then turned and said, "We have to leave."

Reeves's voice crackled over the speakerphone. "I haven't had a chance to ask my own questions."

"Dewey's right. There's no way we can make a return journey in the dark." But Eric remained where he was, and said to Sybille, "What happens to those who don't bond with the players?"

"It's only happened twice that I know of. Plus these two. And the answer is, they're made to vanish." Sybille's features took on a soldier's cast, grim and determined both. "Kathy bonded with me. Which was the first I heard about her using. She was the one who told me about Tyler."

"And now Ryker is hunting me and Tyler," Kathy said. "And when he gets us…"

Sybille continued to stroke the young woman's neck. "That is not going to happen."

By the time Ryker called, Chloe had retreated to her chair behind the desk. Her pacing was drawing attention from the bullpen. Faces rose above the central dividers, like prey peering over the high grass. So she sat and stared out the windows. From time to time she gripped the arms of her chair, forcing herself to stay in place. Waiting had never been this hard.

The setting sun was gradually lost to a rising mist. The golden blanket reformed the buildings and river and bridge and traffic into unified components of an almost mystical light. Chloe noticed that a number of office workers began crowding into empty offices further down the west-facing wall. They pointed and chattered as their world was rendered into something beautiful, something…

Peter bounded into the room. "Anything?"

She gestured to the phone stationed on the middle of her desk. Inert. Silent.

Peter let the door slip shut, crossed the room, and scowled at the phone. It was the expression he used to send a wayward employee into meltdown. Like he could make Ryker call that very instant. Or crush him for disobedience.

When that didn't work, he dropped into the chair. Only then did he notice the people crowded into the adjoining offices. "What's going on over there?"

Chloe waved a hand at the sunset. She half envied these

staffers and their ability to find some shred of wonder from the dusk. When Peter remained silent, she glanced over. He frowned at the employees and their smiling chatter. But not out of irritation. He clearly did not understand what they were doing, or why. Chloe agreed completely.

Her phone rang.

She glanced at the readout. "It's Ryker." She hit the speaker button. "Go."

"The boat's pulling in now."

"Tell me exactly what you see."

"Bannon and the sheriff are seated up front. Bannon is standing now, holding the lines and reaching for the pier. Gator-man is in the pilot's chair. That's pretty much it."

"No sign of anybody else?"

"Just those three."

Peter leaned forward and demanded, "Could the others be hidden somewhere?"

"The boat is open plan." Ryker's raspy whisper was slightly distorted by the phone's speaker. Chloe thought a drone would probably show more emotion. "There's a metal chest between the passenger benches and the pilot's seat. It's about two-thirds the size of a coffin. You might fit somebody in there."

Chloe and Peter exchanged a long look. She waited through half a dozen breaths. Longer. This needed to be his call.

Finally Peter asked, "Can you take them out?"

"Already set it up. There's only one access road to this place. A single-track road runs for about half a mile along the river, then turns left and heads inland. Three-quarters of a mile later, it joins the county highway. The only people on this road are restaurant patrons and locals using the boat slip."

"Sounds ideal," Peter said.

Chloe felt the familiar rush of sending troops into battle. She agreed with Ryker's tactics. If it was going down, this was the place. "Detail it out for us."

"I've brought five of my team. Two are stationed to either side of the bend in the road, ready to take out anyone we miss. Which is highly unlikely. We approach on foot. Offer one final warning. Then we strike."

Chloe asked, "Witnesses?"

"Who's going to believe a bunch of locals describing the impossible?" Ryker might as well have been discussing the weather. "What's more important is, this place is a made-to-order kill zone."

Her boss leaned over the desk and said, "Ryker, your plan is approved. Make it happen."

"Copy that."

But as Peter started to cut the connection, Ryker spoke again. "Hold up a second. We have a newcomer."

Chloe demanded, "Who?"

"Your Air Force buddy just showed up."

"Sybille is there?"

"She sprang out of nowhere. Came around the restaurant's other side, I guess. Okay, now, she's meeting the two lawmen as they come off the pier—"

"Take them out." Peter's voice was as close to savage as a safe little business executive could get. "Under no circumstances are any of them to leave that place alive."

Just in case.

They halted at the furthest boundary of the beach, where five other airboats were moored along the shoreline. Sybille stepped onto the sand, as if joining others watching the sunset. As she pushed the boat back into deep water, Sybille asked why he was putting her off separately. Eric had no answer except those words. Just in case he was right to be worried.

Now she rejoined them as he and Dewey came down the restaurant's long pier. "I haven't seen any sign of danger. Then again, if it's Ryker's crew, I wouldn't."

Eric was about to ask what she meant when there was a soft pattering of footsteps. Eric was facing the crowded parking lot, as alert as he had ever been in his entire life. Even so, he almost missed them. The trio were that fast.

Three shadows slipped across the empty road and joined with the lengthening shadows. There and gone in an instant.

A fourth figure crossed the road at a leisurely pace and started toward them. Eric took the man at mid-thirties, dark-skinned and solid as a wall. He wore denims and a sleeveless sweatshirt, black skullcap, and the sort of canvas boots preferred by desert warriors.

Sybille moaned softly.

It was the oddest conceivable sound to emerge from this

woman, stranger even than the warmth and compassion she had shown Kathy. Eric took it as the only confirmation he needed. Dewey must have read the same memo because he unsnapped the leather catch to his holster and rested his hand on the weapon's grip.

Dewey asked, "That your man?"

Sybille did not respond.

Dewey said, "I make it as three plus the guy here."

Eric thought the same, but he couldn't be sure. The blurs had vanished now, melting into the shadows.

The restaurant was built on chest-high stilts. The row of screened windows all had levered shutters that were wedged a third of the way open. It shaded the interior from the worst of the heat, while allowing in any breath of wind. It also directed the laughter and clattering dishes and jukebox music downwards. As though Eric and the others performed on the sandy stage for an audience seated overhead.

When Ryker slipped through the last line of vehicles, Dewey called, "That's far enough."

Ryker offered them a cheery wave. He looked like any number of special forces Eric had known, an inch or so under six feet and carved from stonelike flesh. There was none of the model's perfectly defined musculature to this man. Everything was functional. Ryker had the look of a seasoned killer, someone who genuinely enjoyed his work.

Ryker said, "You've been a bad girl, Sybille."

His voice was utterly at odds with the rest of him. It reminded Eric of the rush of dead leaves. It was the sound an old man might make, when the last thread of life's force was almost gone, and the power of speech had faded to a sibilant rattle.

"You know what happens to bad girls, don't you, Sybille?" Ryker took a step away from the front line of vehicles. "They get the punishment they deserve."

Dewey unholstered his weapon. "Bud, you just got read your rights."

ROULETTE

* * *

Ryker smiled at Dewey's gun. Like he was watching a comic on the stage. Clearly enjoying himself. "Holster your weapon, cowboy. While your arm is still attached to your body."

A shadow beneath the restaurant emitted a hyena laugh. High-pitched and manic.

Ryker gestured to the restaurant. "I've been ordered to avoid making a scene. So come nice and we'll let you keep breathing."

"That's not happening," Eric said.

"You're wrong about that." Ryker crossed his arms and leaned against a pickup's front fender. Easy and pleasant as his cadaver-voice allowed. "The only question is, are you coming in pieces, or in peace? Get it? Pieces or peace. Pretty good, huh."

This time, Eric heard all three hyenas distinctly. Like falsetto gibberish. "Come any closer and we'll open fire."

"Wrong answer." Ryker smirked at the woman standing to Eric's right. "Tell the man he's making a mistake, Sybille. Save us a lot of pain and bloodshed. Yours too, by the way. All of it."

Sybille was off-tempo. They had agreed she would aim her weapon immediately after Eric issued his warning. Instead, she just stood there with her eyes locked on Ryker. Like trapped prey. Her breathing passed between clenched teeth, and sounded like she was whispering a constant frantic warning.

Ryker clearly enjoyed the woman's terror. "Sybille knows what's coming. She's heard the stories. Gotta love stories. You got any favorite stories, Agent Bannon? Me, I was all about history."

"You don't stand down," said Dewey, "you might just *become* history."

"Sorry, Sheriff. We are the future." The large man took off his skullcap, turning it over in his hands almost thoughtfully. "My favorites were about Viking berserkers. They knew no fear. No pain. You may have heard they would howl like wolves...but did you know they thought they had been changed into animals?

They actually felt they were growing fur. Let's just say we're experiencing a resurgence of the berserkers. But this time we don't settle for make-believe."

Eric glanced at the shadows, but they were still. Ryker's people were listening to his spiel, not using it as a distraction. They didn't need to.

Ryker followed his eyes. "You know how a bird of prey is, trained to eat only from the hawk master's hand. My team eat when I say."

"Last warning," Eric said.

"You took the words right from my mouth." Ryker pushed off the truck. "You ever watched a cat play with its food? My team, they like to start with the hands."

Sybille moaned.

Eric slipped behind her, like she was a stationary dance partner and he was merely shifting position. But when he appeared on her other side, he held her gun. "Another step and you die."

The issue they faced was so common it was remarkable how easily it was overlooked. Even the most seasoned veterans could forget the fact when it stared them in the face.

The basic definition of battle was, *always changing*. In the complexity of combat, with noise and fear and threat and chaos and enemies on every side, identifying something new was extremely difficult.

Eric's own instructors had repeatedly stressed how a battlefield was fluid, never static. As soon as a new tactic was revealed, the enemy was already analyzing. If it proved to be successful, *change accelerated*.

The name for this strategy was taken from biology. It was called *ever-escalating interaction*. When an evolutionary change resulted in a species gaining the upper hand, this success *reinforced* the change and *amplified* the process.

Eric had suspected this was the case ever since Tyler said the shift from human to beast happened more swiftly, and became more controlled, with practice. The question that had to be asked was, change into *what*? Was the beast still evolving? If so, what was the next phase? Because he had to assume the enemy lurking in the restaurant's shadows was much further along this chemically induced shift.

Almost in response to Eric's thinking, Ryker changed.

His transformation took place on a totally different scale from Tyler's. And the change was far more extreme.

All traces of the man were gone.

An ogre stood before them. A giant with a beast's skull. The clothes split and shredded. The hands extended with the talons and the teeth. The eyes were the worst part of him, merciless and yellow-cold.

Ryker snarled.

The sound was loud enough to silence the restaurant. From the sunset-beach behind them, several women screamed. They sounded like prey who had just spotted death's approach.

Sybille joined them, louder and more terrified than all the others combined.

The three came at them from right, left, and straight on. Ryker played the decoy, roaring in their faces.

The trio were instantly on them. There was no time for Eric to raise his weapon, much less take aim and fire. Eric had heard of such speed from lion hunters, who spoke with feverish awe of the animal's attacking force. Eric was a trained agent, had survived action on three continents, and he still could not fire. He could not.

His own assailant was a woman. She landed on Eric's chest and smashed him to the parking lot's broken pavement. She closed her talons on his left thigh and right shoulder, crouched in close enough for him to see the death in her yellow gaze, and snarled.

The pair holding Sybille and Dewey did the same.

The restaurant exploded into one continuous bellow. Sybille seemed capable of shrieking without pausing to draw breath. Eric's entire field of vision was filled with the ogre's face, gleeful and hungry. He heard Ryker's laugh. "Be sure and leave some for me."

Then two shadows flitted across the sky.

On the airboat ride back from the shanty, Eric had actually found the noise helpful.

The battering wind and clamor had fashioned itself into a sunset assault. There was every chance the enemy might be waiting for them. If so, their opponents probably assumed they held all the advantages. They were set up, in position, controlling the terrain. They knew what to expect from their opposition. They had the numbers. They could choose the timing. No doubt they were utterly confident in their ability to attack and annihilate.

Eric intended to use that confidence in his favor.

If Ryker's team were there at all.

His first instructor in tactics had been a student of Sun Tzu, the Chinese general and strategist whose battlefield strategy remained prevalent twenty-five centuries after his death. When facing a stronger force, the lesson went, the leader's first task was not to attack, but…

Unsettle.

Appear when not expected. Create havoc where none existed. Strip away their assumptions. Undermine their strength. Heighten their weakness. Destroy their sense of assurance.

When the riverside restaurant appeared in the distance, Eric signaled to the pilot to cut the motor. They drifted in the golden waters, the air resonating with the sudden silence.

Dewey asked, "What's the matter?"

Eric asked Tyler, "When you're in that state, can you think?"

Tyler nodded, like these were words he had been hoping to hear. "It's very hard."

"Point and shoot," Sybille said. "That's how Ryker always describes his team."

"But somebody has to take aim," Eric said.

Tyler replied, "You're waiting. Like you want somebody to direct."

Kathy added, "Anything to do with the hunt, the prey, that comes natural."

Eric pondered what he was hearing, trying to fit the fragments of an idea together in his head. Their pilot remained motionless in the high chair, hands resting easy on the controls, scouting the waters and the scrubland beyond. Finally Eric asked, "Tyler is linked to Dewey, you're bonded with Sybille, does that alter the way you view each other?"

They looked at each other. "In a way," Kathy said. "We're together, we're friends, but still we're in different..."

"Packs," Tyler said softly.

"Right," Kathy said. "But I trust him."

Dewey clearly hated this conversation. Just hated it. He asked Eric, "Are you going somewhere with this?"

"Maybe." Eric asked Kathy, "What happens if, say, I went after Sybille?"

"Don't," she replied. "Please."

"Or if Dewey were to attack—"

"*Stop.*" This time both young people spoke together. Tyler added, "It hurts my head."

"You can't ask that." Kathy panted softly. "It's *wrong.*"

The pilot spat over the gunnel and said, "None of you's making any sense, you know that, don't you?"

Eric leaned back, satisfied. "Actually, it makes all the sense in the world."

The beast that had been Tyler Brock roared as he flew—*flew*—down from his rooftop perch.

He leapt with hands and feet outstretched, talons arched, mouth filled with canine incisors. His eyes were slanted, yellow, and furious.

The roars that now resonated through the parking lot no longer all belonged to Ryker's pack.

The beast holding Dewey to the pavement lifted his head, or started to. But Tyler was on him too fast. Tyler *hammered* the assailant.

The woman holding Eric was momentarily distracted. She peered about, and then she…

Mewed.

She craned about so as to observe Tyler and the beast who had held Dewey spin across the pavement. They fought and rolled with the speed of cats fighting, only larger and louder and meaner.

Then Kathy struck the beast imprisoning Sybille. Her timing was perfect. The attacker pinning Sybille was busy watching as Ryker leapt into the struggle against Tyler. Kathy slammed the third assailant so hard he shot across the free space in front of the restaurant's entrance and struck a panel truck, caving in the side. Kathy was instantly on him, pounding his head against the truck. Each blow deepened the dent.

Eric bucked as hard as he could. She released one claw so as to maintain her balance.

The shift was enough for Eric to dislodge his gun arm.

How he had managed to keep hold of Sybille's weapon was a credit to his training. His shoulder was numb from where her talons had dug into the flesh and his hand would not raise more than a few inches off the earth. But it was enough to press the nozzle into her side.

He fired.

She was knocked off and to his left.

The pain in Eric's shoulder and thigh only really started then, when he was free and moving. Standing would take too long, he could tell that much. And his right arm felt lashed to the pavement. So he reached across with his left arm, and only then realized the gun was slick with his own blood.

The woman pounced.

She slammed him back down, crushing the air from his lungs. Eric sucked in breath, wheezed against the pressure on his ribcage. Flailing, he kicked out. Her weight lifted momentarily, long enough for Eric to gasp a single breath. Then she hammered both sides of his head. His ears exploded with pain, ringing.

Her face lowered to where all Eric saw were the yellow eyes. The fury. Her claws began sinking into his cheek, his temple, his skull. Eric's window of vision began narrowing, closing.

Then Dewey fired.

And fired. And fired.

Even when mortally wounded, Eric's captor remained impossibly fast. She scrambled and weaved and howled, a predator hunting for cover. Dewey followed her, firing steadily, tracking her like the trained lawman that he was.

The beast slowed, slumped, and finally went still.

Ryker and the other beasts paused as well. And bellowed higher and louder than ever before.

As he struggled to rise, Eric realized he had made a terrible mistake. Up to that point, he had still considered them as merely *changed*. That they were still *human*. But there was nothing human left in that howl of shared anguish.

Tyler and his two foes fought their way down the next line of parked vehicles, breaking windows and setting off car alarms.

Eric wiped blood from his face, aimed at the beast battling it out with Kathy, and pulled the trigger. The gun clicked empty.

"*Eric! Here!*" Sybille was unable to stand, but her upraised hand held a fresh clip.

He reloaded and limped forward. Dewey was over to Eric's right, firing every time one of Tyler's assailants gave him a clean shot. Eric was shooting left-handed. He moved as fast as he could, closing the distance, determined to take out their leader. His eyes stung with sweat—he hoped it was sweat—and his vision was still not fully clear.

Ryker lifted his head, glared at Dewey, and...

Barked.

It was a new sound, one that froze Eric momentarily. The force of command was there in the noise. An officer demanding obedience from his team.

The two remaining beasts howled in fury and frustration, but immediately they...

Ran.

Eric got off four more shots, but he doubted any of them struck home. The other attacker who had been on Tyler appeared to be limping, but it was hard to tell. They moved that fast.

Tyler and Kathy started to give chase. Dewey shouted first, then Sybille. Before the names were fully formed, the three attackers were gone.

Only then did Eric hear the screams rising from the restaurant.

The airboat pilot had done his job perfectly.

Dewey's instructions prior to docking had been military terse. Record the entire incident on Eric's cellphone, starting with their walk down the pier. The restaurant was only a few miles from the nearest cell tower, so outside contact was a cinch. Hank was also instructed to use Dewey's phone to call 911, say the sheriff faced incoming fire, and add, *officer down.*

Eric had to assume by that point those two words would most likely be true.

As soon as the action reached a natural pause, assuming there was any action at all, Hank was to send his video feed to the last number Eric had called.

Howls from the three remaining attackers continued to reverberate long after they had vanished into the scrubland. Eric and Sybille gathered up Kathy while Dewey went for Tyler. Eric stripped off his shirt and settled it over the head of the felled attacker. She had returned to a human form now, bent and battered and very dead. But human.

Together they limped down the long pier to where the airboat was moored.

Meanwhile the restaurant underwent a manic evacuation. People shouted and children shrieked and horns blew and engines revved. Several dozen vehicles, most of them pickups, fought for the exit. Dust hung heavy in the still air, turned crimson by the final light of day. Departing airboats roared into the distance.

Hank released the lines holding them to the dock and positioned his airboat about a hundred meters downstream. The sandy beach was empty now. The river was wide at this point, which meant the water was very slow moving. The pilot handed Sybille a battered toolbox holding his first-aid kit. She and Dewey treated first Eric and then Tyler, while Hank used a long-handled oar to keep them in place. The pilot's gaze continually shifted from Tyler and Kathy back to the empty shore.

Eventually a burly man in a stained chef's apron stepped onto the patio holding a long-barrel rifle. He called down, "Sheriff, what's going on out there?"

"Get back inside, Kevin! Did you call 911?"

"'Bout fifty times. Won't do no good, though. Can't nobody get down here. Not with all my customers and half my staff jamming the access road."

"Man's got a point," Hank said.

"You're safe enough," Dewey called back. "We're staying right here until help arrives. Now go back inside and lock your place down."

When the restaurant owner retreated, Hank said, "Don't see as how a door would keep them things out of anywhere they wanted to go."

Dewey's response was to take up position in the bow. He scanned the perimeter, the pilot's twelve-gauge loaded and cocked in his hands.

Hank said, "Don't suppose it'd do me any good to ask what it was I saw back there."

Sybille sat on the middle bench, one arm around each of the two young people. They huddled in close to her sides, drawing from her strength and warmth.

Hank said, "No, I figured it wouldn't."

Eric stood on the platform holding the pilot's chair, his gaze fastened farther out, watching the lengthening shadows for any sign of movement.

Dewey shifted the shotgun to one arm. "Hank, hand me that phone, let me see what's holding up the authorities." He dialed, spoke softly, then set the phone on the bench behind him. "Chopper is still thirty minutes out."

"It'll be full dark by then," Hank fretted. "Wouldn't give us much of a chance, taking on them critters at night."

"We'll shift over to the restaurant in a bit," Dewey said. "Have them turn on the floodlights."

Hank spat over the rail. "Don't reckon the restaurant's gonna improve our prospects much neither."

Eric waited through another five minutes, long enough to grow fairly certain the beasts had used the restaurant's evacuation as cover for their own withdrawal. Ryker was former special forces, according to Sybille, which was where he had linked up with Chloe. Ryker would know the sheriff's alerts would result in reinforcements headed their way. It was time for a good officer to cut his losses and protect his remaining crew.

Which was precisely what Eric had in mind.

He said, "We need to plan."

Dewey remained intent on the floodlit restaurant grounds. "Maybe we should do that inside the building."

"In a minute." He turned to Sybille. "I'm going to run through a what if. You need to decide how you want it to play out."

She did not meet Eric's gaze. "I let you down back there."

Dewey must have expected the comment, for he responded without halting his scan. "If I had known what we were gonna be facing, I'd have been spooked out of my skin."

"Pretty much did that to me, and I still don't know what I saw," Hank agreed.

"That was then and this is now," Eric said. "Here's what you need to focus on. The Pentagon is a cavern. Massive and conflicted. There is competition between senior officers, between special forces and general troops, between each of the military arms. Right up to the Joint Chiefs. Fighting for attention, money, positioning, or just fighting. Do you understand what I'm saying?"

Sybille was watching him now. As were the two young people. And Hank. Only Dewey kept his gaze aimed on the gradually dimming shoreline.

"Back at the shanty, when I called Ambassador Reeves and he spoke with you, I imagine he had already gathered a half-dozen people. They were all crammed into his White House office," Eric went on. "Allies within military intelligence and senior command. People who might even have heard rumors of your operation, but were lacking sufficient proof to take action. People who were genuinely worried. People who would be opposed to any such action on the grounds of common sense and human decency. People who stood ready to do whatever it takes to shut it all down, just as soon as they received evidence strong enough to release them from needing to run this up the chain of command."

Sybille opened her mouth but did not speak.

Dewey asked, "You think this, or you know?"

"I am absolutely certain it's happened, based on serving with Reeves for over a decade. But I have no evidence."

Dewey nodded slowly. "Works for me."

Eric pointed to the south. "The Naval Air Arm is located ninety miles away, close to the University of Central Florida's main campus. Soon as Hank made the call and passed on the video feed showing Reeves that the attack was on, I am certain the ambassador's allies scrambled teams that they had already put on alert."

Sybille tasted the air, asked, "How long do we have?"

"Ten minutes," Eric said. "Maybe less."

Hank said, "A few gunships lighting up this place sounds good to me."

Eric said, "Soon as they arrive, we lose control. Do you understand what I'm saying?"

Sybille sat up straighter. "Kathy."

"And Tyler. They'll be taken into custody. And studied."

Tyler asked, "You mean, locked up?"

"Look at it this way," Eric replied. "What could they possibly gain by ever letting you go free?"

Chloe cut the connection and rose from her chair. Dusk had settled now, and the offices facing the sunset splendor had emptied out. Even with Peter watching and waiting for her report, she felt no need to hurry. Not any longer. At a visceral level she considered this to be the fate she had been destined for. Surrounded by the impossible pressures of a project gone totally off the grid.

She wrapped her arms around her chest. Squeezing herself so tightly she had to fight against her own strength just to breathe. She had to think. She had to *focus*.

Peter rose from his chair. She could see his reflection in the darkening glass. His legs appeared scarcely able to carry him across the room. "Did Ryker just say he lost one of his team?"

Chloe nodded slowly. Not to Peter. But rather to her own internal dialogue.

It was over.

Peter moved in closer. "Ryker *lost*?"

We all did, was what she thought. But there was no profit in saying the words aloud.

No future.

Chloe turned around and forced herself to play the capable executive. "We need to plan."

"Plan? Ryker's team was our secret weapon! And he just got taken out!"

"Which means everything needs to speed up," Chloe said. She walked around her office, knelt, and opened the credenza. An oblong safe occupied the entire lower shelf. She pressed her thumb into the print reader. When it pinged, she punched in the code and opened the door. The safe's only contents was a leather briefcase. She pulled it out and set it on the desk. "Do you have an escape plan?"

"Do I...Are you even hearing yourself?"

"Yes, Peter. And you need to realize, the game is over."

"No...You don't get to say that." Peter swiped his forehead. The sweat and electric fear frayed his careful preppy composure. "Ryker lost only one of his team. We can still make this work."

Chloe was two people now. One part of her, the major part, worked through the coming scenarios. Charting her course. Because she had to hold to a precise course, or she would lose...

Everything.

The smaller portion played the subordinate. Talking her boss down off the ceiling. Clarifying the new reality. "It doesn't matter how many of Ryker's team are left, Peter. You know why? Because this is the point at which our superiors in Washington are going to cut their losses. We promised them a new soldier. One which was essentially invulnerable."

"No, wait—"

"We also promised them something else." She opened her briefcase, unlocked the drawer, and began transferring the contents. Everything except for one article went into her case. "I hope you're listening because this is where our situation moves from serious to critical. We promised them that we would keep our experimental trials under the radar. And we failed."

Peter stared at her across the desk, the shock of realization turning his gaze hollow.

She slipped the final item into her pocket. "There is only one response to failure of this scale, Peter. Liquidation. Severing all ties. Reducing their risk of discovery. Which will happen if anybody survives and turns state's evidence."

He shuddered so violently he might have been entering convulsions. Chloe had often wondered how Peter would respond if the forces he played with actually drew him into the maelstrom. Now she knew.

She closed the drawer and snapped the catches on her case. "You have a bolt hole, don't you, Peter? A secret safe haven."

He needed three tries to shape the word, "Belize."

"And your escape package. New ID, traveling cash, maybe a weapon. Where do you keep that?"

"House."

"Here is better, Peter. Keep it where you spend most of your time. You'll remember that next time, won't you?" She hefted the case, rounded her desk, and took her boss by the arm. Keeping her voice steady and her pace slow. Resisting the urge to scream at him, drag him down the hall, shriek in his ear that they were all going to die. Nothing to be gained from that. Nothing at all.

Chloe led him from the office and along the side corridor and over to the elevators. When the doors slid shut and they were alone once more, she went on, "So we'll go by your place and pick up your stuff. Then we'll take your plane. You're divorced, and that's a good thing, since it reduces the risk of collateral damage."

She ignored his renewed shudder as she pulled out her phone and hit the speed dial for the company's travel department. There was someone on duty twenty-four seven, a perk that Peter had always treated as his due. Chloe had considered it just another opportunity for her boss to enjoy an ego massage. Until now.

When the travel desk answered, she said, "I'm calling for Peter Sandling. He wants the jet prepped and ready to depart in half an hour." She handed him the phone and said softly, "Tell the lady just how urgent this is." When he just stared at her, she added, "Lives depend on you getting this right."

Peter managed the call, but the words were fractured by shudders that would not stop. When the elevator doors opened, Chloe realized he would never make it on his own. She wrapped the arm not holding her briefcase around his shoulders and steered him out. By the time they passed the reception desk and the guard on evening duty, she was supporting most of his weight. Chloe said something about Peter being taken ill. The guard responded with words she did not even bother to hear.

The night air encased them in a soft humid blanket. Peter revived enough to say, "I can do this."

"Of course you can." Even so, she maintained a grip on his arm as they turned left at the parking lot and stopped by Peter's Ferrari. She released her hold as he opened the door, then asked, "Maybe I should drive."

Peter hesitated, then decided, "Good idea."

"I'll run into your home, pick up your go bag." When Peter's only response was another trembly nod, she lied, "I'll need your combination."

"Four-four-seven-nine-nine."

Which confirmed what she already knew. Chloe shepherded him around the car. She waited until he was doing the swoop-and-dive required to enter the car's low seat. Then she extracted the item that had not gone into her briefcase.

As Peter settled into the passenger seat, she uncapped the pen and touched the tip to his neck.

Within a couple of seconds, Peter felt the drug's impact. He jerked with the shock, or tried to. "No, wait, why…"

"Because it's my only hope of survival." Chloe squatted down beside him. "Because they will demand a sacrifice. Maybe by offering you up like this, they'll let me go. It's not much of a hope, but it's all I have."

The drug wrapped a thin veil over his gaze. "But, you…"

"They'll show up here with a full attack squad. Everybody in suits, carrying badges, ready for a frontal assault against your security. Instead, here you are, all wrapped up like a Christmas package." Chloe tapped the pen to his bare skin once more. A third time. Fourth. Fifth. And a final tap for good measure.

She rose to her feet. "Hopefully this will at least slow them down."

Two weeks later

They took a Southwest flight from Orlando to Washington-Reagan. Carol and Dewey had never been to Washington before, and Stacie had only visited as a child. Eric enjoyed playing tour guide. They stayed at the Mayflower Hotel on Connecticut, compliments of the White House. Carol and Dewey had a suite and Eric and Stacie were given luxury rooms farther down the same hall.

They were granted a day to visit the Mall and the monuments and the museums. Over a picnic lunch by the central pool, Stacie released the unspoken worry Eric knew she had been carrying since that day in the hospital. "What if, you know, I have another episode?"

"I don't think you will," he replied. "When was the last time you felt the internal shift?"

"El Comandante's office." She smiled at Carol. "You and Lauren were right about that visit. It was fun. Twisted, but fun."

"Benny Benitez is a turkey," Carol said. "He desperately needed the basting you gave him."

Eric said, "So two weeks without a whisper. That suggests the remnants of the drug and the attack might be wearing off."

"But what if, you know…"

"I will be there. For you." He hesitated, then added, "If you want."

When they emerged the next morning, a Cadillac Escalade was parked by the hotel's entrance. An Air Force corporal leapt from the driver's seat and snapped off a salute. "Agent Bannon?"

"Right person, wrong title," Eric replied.

"Sir, I'm instructed to deliver you to ground zero."

"These three people are coming with me."

"Sir, as far as my orders go, you're welcome to be accompanied by the Naval Academy's marching band." He held the front passenger door for Dewey. "The Pentagon's entire transport detail has been ordered to stay ready for any request you or your associates might care to make. Most incredible orders it's ever been my pleasure to hear. You should've seen the bugs swarm."

Eric insisted on taking the middle position between the two women. When they were underway, Dewey turned in his seat and said, "Y'all comfortable back there?"

"Absolutely," Carol said. "I don't have a thing against being tucked in tight beside a handsome secret agent man."

When Stacie hummed her agreement, Dewey asked, "Anything we need to know about your boss?"

They had been over this the previous evening, but Eric had no problem repeating himself. He knew they were still coming to terms with traveling to the hurricane's eye. He replied, "Ambassador Reeves prefers to receive the raw intel and draw his own conclusions. Tell him what you experienced, what you heard and saw, what you know. Then stop."

Carol asked, "So what's he like really, your boss?"

"Pretty much the same as everybody else working on Pennsylvania Avenue," Eric replied. "They're some of the best in the world at their job. They're also intense, stressed, and experts at playing the political system."

Stacie asked, "How would you handle what's coming?"

Eric replied, "Be honest, direct, and to the point. Never use two words when one will do."

"You've just defined my husband," Carol said.

Eric added, "Treat this meeting as if our lives hang in the balance."

This time, the corporal laughed out loud.

The driver pulled up on Seventeenth Street, and a young staffer rushed down the stairs to greet them. Eric cautioned, "Remember, stay focused, stay alert."

Although its official name was now the Eisenhower Building, most occupants of the wedding-cake structure fronting 17th Street still referred to it as the OEOB. The staffer guided them through the sign-in and vetting and security inspection, then passed around visitor badges. They climbed the grand staircase and walked down a corridor whose tiled floor weaved gently on the currents of centuries. The staffer knocked softly on an oiled mahogany door, opened it, and said, "They're here."

As soon as Eric entered, he knew he had been right to say nothing about what they would face. What had originally been a formal reception hall now held a polished oval table that could have comfortably seated thirty. A trio of chandeliers illuminated walls rimmed in mahogany wainscoting. Every branch of the military was represented. Eric counted three generals, an admiral, and six colonels seated around the table's far end. Twice that number of aides lined the side and rear walls. The three people among them wearing civilian suits all exuded the grey, diffident air of senior intelligence bureaucrats. They were professionals at showing little and saying less. They would watch the Presidential appointees come and go from the safety of quiet offices one floor below the director's level. Down where the real work was done, the analyses prepared, the decisions made over who went where and did what. In total secrecy.

The room's occupants greeted Eric's arrival with stony silence.

The best one-word description for Eric's boss was *square*. A cubic head was planted atop a square neck attached to a rectangular body. Even his spectacles were square. At seventy-one, Ambassador Reeves remained one of the most energetic and driven men Eric had ever met. He shook each of their hands and solemnly thanked them for coming. As if they had been given any choice.

Once they were seated and offers of drinks had been declined, Reeves requested that they give a detailed overview of everything they had experienced. Dewey went first, then Carol, then Stacie. All three held to the clipped, nervous voices of people rendered very disconcerted by their surroundings. Which was a big reason why Eric had not offered them any warning about what they would probably be facing here. He wanted them to appear precisely as they were now. Uncoached. Raw. Inexperienced at the Washington-type games this group had probably expected.

Reeves asked each of them a few questions in turn, drawing out details that they had skipped over. He then turned to Eric and said, "Your turn."

Eric gave it to them blow-by-blow. He had no notes. When he was done, he went silent. And waited.

Reeves said, "Now give us your assessment."

Up to this point, the brass had been silent. The admiral, one of the few women at the table, said, "I'd like somebody to tell me why we were kept waiting two weeks for this meeting."

Eric's gaze remained locked on Reeves.

Reeves ignored the admiral and repeated, "Your assessment. Go."

The research Eric had managed to pull together pointed to the same thing: It all came down to emergent behavior.

That term, *emergent behavior,* was defined as actions by a group that did not originate from any one individual.

Specialists in group dynamics considered this a low-level code, created during early stages of biological development.

As in, *genetic* development.

Emergent behavior had been observed in virtually every life form on earth, from swarming termites to the complex social structures of early human societies. Flocking birds were a perfect example. No one bird was designated as a leader. There was not a definite mental structure that told them to fly in an arrow-like formation. Instead, the rules were extremely simple, so straightforward that they could be reduced to a level of genes and muscle and sinew. Fly and don't touch other birds, but stay close. All animals threatened by carnivores flocked so that any one animal's risk of being attacked was reduced.

In short, emergent behavior was defined by rules so rigid and simple, observers could not even say if they were dictated by the brain, or biologically hardwired.

Which was where Eric's assessment moved from science to conjecture.

Eric figured that when Palindrome's research shifted to human test subjects, the laws of emergent behavior resulted in unwanted results. These outcomes could not be altered because they were not learned behavior. They were designed into the core nature of the test subject. At the genetic level.

Given what he had witnessed, with Tyler and Kathy and Ryker's team, Eric was fairly certain the crisis issue came down to *bonding*.

As in, who controlled the newly enhanced warrior.

And who controlled the controller.

The admiral was a spare woman, all sinew and steam. Even her gaze was smoky. She interrupted with, "I'm still waiting for an answer to my question."

Reeves turned and frowned at her. Eric knew that expression all too well. Ambassador Reeves had the ability to reduce the most powerful people to an embarrassing stain.

She shifted nervously under the weight of his iron-hard gaze. "Well?"

Reeves merely turned back to Eric and said, "Please continue."

Anthropologists had long wondered about the role of medicine men in primitive society. Cave paintings that predated the advent of written language hinted at a universal aspect of hunting rituals, a shared experience that transcended cultural and racial boundaries.

Scientists then pointed to the need for modern-day warriors to require a single leader to be in charge of them when they entered high-threat situations. Frontline troops tended to respond best when they only heard one trusted voice. In many cases, this was the only way a group could be ensured to follow orders. Insert a second commander, and a highly trained unit was often reduced to the behavioral level of a kindergarten class. They might do as they were instructed. But they were equally liable to follow an outside stimulus, and head off in an unscripted direction, and die as a result.

Studies of human behavior in high-risk, high-stress environments suggested there was some elemental component of human genetic makeup that had been suppressed in modern man. It was a factor of emergent behavior, not taught, but rather hardwired into what was now called the *warrior syndrome.*

In every test subject, this focus on their leader, or medicine man, was paramount. They lost the ability to heed orders from anyone else. They became, in effect, weapons that only responded to one voice imprint.

Which meant if the controller went rogue, the entire group became just another enemy.

Eric assumed this prospect had wrecked the outcome. The project was cancelled. The research was deemed radioactive. The entire lab team was given an ultimatum. Stay quiet, forget everything, or vanish.

At least, that was the official version.

But for some inside the Pentagon, the lure of super-warriors was too great.

These Pentagon officials hoped that perhaps, over time, a *second* bonding might take place.

So they continued the study. In secret. At arm's length.

Which the Jacksonville company was only too happy to do. It was one thing to be gagged because of failure. And another thing entirely for such a major discovery to be shredded because the investors—in this case, military intelligence—disliked one minor aspect of the result.

Or perhaps not so minor.

Ambassador Reeves accepted Eric's summary with a nod, then turned to the gathered brass and said, "Questions?"

"It's about time," the admiral said.

"Let's make one thing perfectly clear," Reeves added. "We are here because members of the military went rogue."

The admiral bridled. "Not from my branch."

The lone Air Force general said, "We've already covered that."

"As far as the Senate's appropriation and intelligence committees are concerned," Reeves replied, "you will be painted with the same brush. All of you."

The admiral glared at Reeves, but did not respond.

He asked a second time, "Questions?"

The Air Force general said, "Let's cut to the chase."

"Roger that," one of the Army brass said.

"We all want to know the same three things. First, where are the people responsible? Second, where are the remaining…"

"Beasts," Eric said. "I don't know any word that works better."

"And third, when can our scientists get their hands on the drugs and the survivors?"

"And the data," an Army brass added. "No need to repeat their field work."

Stacie glared at the other end of the table. "Do you even hear yourselves?"

"We'll answer them in reverse order," Eric said. "The compound where the drug was produced and distributed has been located in an isolated region of central Florida."

The admiral said, "Define isolated."

"No roads. Predators. Swamp. Bugs. Heavy brush. Diseases for which there is no known cure."

"Snakes," Dewey added. "Wild pigs. Locals who are only too willing to make outsiders vanish."

Eric said, "The sheriff's office used data gathered by Air Force drones to pinpoint the compound."

Dewey said, "We limited the search to scrublands between Jacksonville and Ocala. Even so, that totaled over three hundred thousand acres. Too much for the regional authorities to cover. We couldn't have done it without your help."

Eric said, "Down in Florida, an illegal drug factory is known as a grow house. It gives off a recognizable signature. One or more high-powered generators. A chemical dump."

"Barracks often hidden underground," Dewey said. "No matter how carefully they insulate, we'll usually be able to detect a major heat signature."

Eric nodded to Stacie, who drew a file from her shoulder bag. She passed it to Eric, who slid it across to Reeves. "The compound was raided. We found numerous confirmations that this served both as the lab and the team's safe house."

Dewey said, "One of those photos shows a military-style training area. Have a look at the claw marks on all those poles."

Eric said, "The lab had already been demolished when Dewey's team arrived. But the barrels of refuse chemicals you see there have been analyzed and compared to lab documents recovered from Palindrome. They contained specific waste chemicals resulting from the production of Labellan."

The Air Force general demanded, "In what quantities?"

"We'll have to get back to you on that." Reeves rolled his finger. Move on. "Second point."

Dewey said, "So far, we have identified no evidence directly linking Palindrome or any of its employees to the illegal lab. We've brought in state and federal prosecutors. They do not feel there is sufficient proof to arrest anyone."

Eric said, "Peter Sandling, Palindrome's CEO, was found dead at his corporate headquarters. We have to assume it was a suicide. No note has been identified."

"Convenient," the Air Force general said.

Dewey said, "Dr. Swann and my wife apprehended the missing Palindrome scientist, Dr. Kevin Lassiter. Soon after he was taken into custody, he died. Evidence of foul play is sketchy, but we suspect he was executed."

Reeves allowed the silence to gather and bear down.

Finally the top Army general demanded, "When do we get our hands on the drugs and those test subjects?"

"You don't," Reeves replied.

The rumbling growing at the table's far end sounded to Eric as though the brass were verbally preparing for war. Only the civilians kept still.

"Utter one complaint," Reeves said. "Make one protest of any kind. Show any indication that you are seeking to enter what is now a forbidden zone. The President has issued written orders. Your branch's intel budget will be decimated."

The other end of the table appeared to have lost the ability to breathe.

Reeves rose to his feet. "This briefing is now concluded. Everything to do with this incident is now classed as radioactive. Discussing this with anyone outside this room will render your careers history. You are dismissed."

The Eisenhower Building was connected to the White House by way of a tunnel that ran beneath the main parking area. A Marine on sentry duty in the basement foyer inspected their IDs and passes, then called ahead to confirm they were expected.

They were accompanied by a silent, grey-suited civilian woman who had been seated with the brass. Reeves took them on a roundabout tour of several public rooms, granting them a little time to gawk, but checking his watch on occasion. When it was time, he led them out a pair of French doors. A porticoed walk ran partway down the building, bordered by rose bushes in full bloom. Reeves stopped by a trio of wrought-iron benches. "Why don't you make yourselves comfortable? We may be here awhile."

Carol hugged herself, as excited as Eric had ever seen her. She demanded, "You knew this was happening?"

"Not until this very moment," he replied. "I asked. And got no response."

The ambassador replied, "Because we weren't sure we could make it work."

Dewey offered Eric the now-familiar cop smile. "Okay, so maybe I owe you one."

"Not now, not ever," Eric replied.

Stacie stepped in close enough to speak so no one else could hear them. "Come over here for a second."

Eric allowed Stacie to draw him further down the walk, toward where another Marine stood sentry. Stacie Swann possessed a distinct intensity that kept the world at an analytical arm's length. Eric doubted she was even aware of the energy that surrounded her. For now, however, her barriers were removed. Eric watched how the sunlight played a copper melody through her dark hair and turned the grey eyes into a rich golden smoke. Her makeup was so subtle as to go unnoticed, but from this close he detected a faint splash of freckles that adorned both cheeks. Matter of fact, he would be happy to stand there all day.

She addressed her words to the traffic sweeping beyond the emerald-gold lawn, "I keep waiting for you to make a wrong move."

"Excuse me?"

"I don't mean professionally. You're very good at your job and all that. I mean, as a man. As a friend. As..."

Eric could see she was struggling. He wanted to help. But when he opened his mouth, no sound emerged. He could not even put together a decent thought.

"I've had some truly awful relationships. So bad I'm actually embarrassed when I think about..." She shook her head, dismissing the unfinished sentence. "I've learned to expect so little from my private life. And then here you come."

Eric was filled with a sudden urge to shout just as loud as he possibly could and order the world to stop turning. Keep this moment alive for an impossible length of time. Freeze the instant, keep hold of it, forever if possible.

She said, "I need to ask you something. This is real, isn't it?"

Thankfully, he regained the power of speech. "Yes."

"I'm talking about us."

"I know. The answer is the same."

She sighed. All the tension just slipped away, leaving her shoulders slumped. She looked so sad. So vulnerable. "I want this to be different. So much."

"Stacie...Can you look at me?"

She kept her gaze on the rear garden. "This is the wrong time and place, I know. But I needed to ask. While I had the courage."

"Stacie. Please."

She turned to him. He could see tears gathered at the edges of her eyes. The pinched mouth, the taut features, the grip she kept on her arms crossing her middle. An inch away from losing control. So afraid. So desperate.

He said the only thing that seemed right. "This moment, what you've just said, is our first anniversary. Twenty years from now, I'm still going to owe you flowers."

She did not move for a very long moment. Then one hand jerked free and rose to swipe at her eyes. "I've wondered for years if maybe I didn't deserve a man who would bring me roses."

He said, "I wish I could kiss you."

Her response was cut off by Reeves calling his name. "Heads-up, everyone. We're on."

Even with the Secret Service emerging at the corridor's far end, even with the phalanx of dark-suited power that started toward them, still Stacie took the time to scald Eric with an extremely heated, very feminine look.

Reeves arranged them into a line with their backs to the rose garden. As Reeves introduced them, each received a brief handshake and a few words. Until, that is, Reeves came to the last in line and said, "And this is Stacie Swann."

The President of the United States gave her a closer inspection, then said, "Ambassador Reeves tells me you are going to be of considerable service to our country."

"She already has been, Mr. President," Reeves said.

He nodded. "I expect great things from you, Dr. Swann."

Then he was gone.

Reeves clapped his hands. "What say we get to work."

***

They entered a remarkably small office, scarcely large enough to hold the antique desk, a sofa, a coffee table, and two straight-back chairs. But the view was over the front lawn, out to where the hordes stared through the wrought-iron fence. The hall behind them resonated with the quiet rush of global power.

Reeves directed Eric and Stacie to the chairs opposite his desk. Dewey and Carol stood in the doorway. The ambassador slid a file across to Eric. "This should do it."

Eric glanced over the two pages it contained, then nodded his thanks to the ambassador.

The first page was a letter of commendation signed by both the Director of Homeland Security and the President of the United States. Thanking Dr. Stacie Swann for her contribution to national security and the sacrifices she endured to avert a potential disaster. The final paragraph was a formal commendation regarding her professional qualifications.

The second page was an official request, signed by the US Surgeon General, appointing Stacie as director of a new lab to be established in conjunction with the UF teaching hospital and genetics laboratories. Her duties, if she were to accept this directorship, were to be defined as she went along. Her budget was effectively without ceiling. She was to answer directly to the Surgeon General and no one else.

Eric passed the file to Stacie. "This is for you."

Chloe only stayed in Belize long enough to raid Peter's stash.

She felt surprisingly little guilt over having fed her boss to the federal wolves. And none whatsoever over robbing him blind.

After all, it wasn't like he was ever going to need it.

She took the Palindrome jet straight to the island resort. She had flown on the corporate bus enough for no one to question her traveling alone. As requested, Peter's resident steward was there planeside to greet her. When she entered the hilltop palace, she was tempted to stay. But there was too much risk involved, too great a chance the feds would come hunting.

Chloe had stolen all of Peter's security codes within a month of her arrival, a throwback to her days in the field. At the time, it had seemed somewhat obsessive, readying herself to rob the guy who had lured her into civilian life. But as she pried open the safe and found a massive stash of cash, bearer bonds, gold, and diamonds, Chloe decided a little obsession was not such a bad trait after all.

She returned to the jet and set two wrapped bundles of cash on the console between the pilots. "Twenty thousand dollars to fly me to Nicaragua and make a false record of your destination."

The pilots might as well have prepped all day for her offer. The captain neither blinked nor hesitated. "Twenty each."

She was ready for that as well. Chloe plunked down another

two bundles and said, "I want to be airborne in five minutes or less."

Managua was the pits. The capital city's best hotel, the Real Metrocenter, was a museum in desperate need of refurbishment. Or a wrecking ball, she couldn't decide which. The penthouse suite offered her a balcony view of the chaotic traffic and the polluted lake beyond. Soon as she entered, she called down for a meal and the hotel manager. They arrived together. As she ate, she offered a sizeable gift to the director's retirement fund in exchange for a private meeting with Nicaragua's most powerful attorney. Here. In her suite. Within the hour.

The manager came through as only a five-star hotel director could. The lawyer arrived with a cohort of six aides, all billable to Chloe by the hour. She did not care. They came. That was the important issue.

The manager clearly wanted to stay, and she was fine with that as well. "I want Nicaraguan citizenship, passport, incorporation, the works."

The senior attorney was handsome as a silver fox and dressed in Saville Row's finest. "We can certainly assist you in all those manners, madame."

"And I want it immediately. Without delay."

He had clearly fielded such a request before. "Time, as they say, is money. The less you have, the more it will cost you."

She opened one of the heavy parchment envelopes and allowed a fistful of Peter's Belize diamonds to spill on the table between them. "I want you to sell these, pay your fees, grease the appropriate hands, and bank the rest in the account of my new company."

"It will be my pleasure." He swept a hand across the leather-topped table, scooped up the gemstones, then reached out for the envelope. "And the name of your new group?"

"Survival, Incorporated." She waved a hand. "I'm not done. Dismiss your troops."

When it was just the two of them, she went on, "I need a safe haven."

"Madame, I assure you, Nicaragua has never honored its extradition treaty with the United States. And a woman of your means will most certainly not become the test case."

"Maybe not, but I can't stay here."

"May I ask why not?"

"No."

He leaned back. "What did you have in mind?"

Describing what she wanted required less than ninety seconds.

He rose to his feet, patted his immaculate hair, and smiled. "In that case, there isn't a moment to lose."

The Chinese ambassador's coterie was so large they filled every seat in Chloe's penthouse parlor. More stood around the walls with the attorney's six aides. The ambassador did not introduce them. She was an elegant woman in her early sixties, with the regal coldness of a royal assassin. If she objected in any way to Chloe's summons, she did not show it. After refusing the offer of refreshments, she said in perfect English, "I am here."

"I want to show you the results of human experiments that took place under the auspices of the Department of Defense."

"First you will tell me what you want," the woman said.

"Protection," Chloe replied. "My enemies know what I have in my possession. They can't afford to let me live. I need friends who will keep me safe."

"You have the technology related to what you are about to show me?"

"The data, the test results, the formula, everything." Chloe gave that a beat, then added, "And more."

"More?"

"What you're about to see. They are mine."

The woman surprised her then. There was no sign of any doubt. No hesitation. Nor did the ambassador ask for any sort of clarification. Instead, she merely said, "Very well. Show."

Instead, Chloe said, "You know what I have here, don't you?"

"You think this research would go unnoticed? Of course I know."

"And you know about me."

"You, your background, your recent…"

"Escape," Chloe said.

The woman had a terrible smile. A mere rearranging of the lower half of her face. No mirth, no warmth, no assurance of any kind. "Your test subjects are safe?"

"They are."

"We will have access to them?"

"Perhaps. First you'll need to convince us of their freedom."

The woman nodded. "Not safety."

"Safety is not really an issue here. Freedom is."

"But you lost one of them in a firefight, correct?"

"They aren't invulnerable. But they are very impressive."

"Can they be controlled?"

"They are bonded to their leader, and he is bonded to me."

"Bonded?"

"Right." Chloe started to explain about the explosive charge embedded in each right arm. The same sort of charge she had used to take out the lab technician, their last remaining loose end. But some secrets could wait. "Do we have a deal?"

The woman offered her another chilling smile. "Show."

THOMAS LOCKE is the pen-name of Davis Bunn, whose novels have sold in excess of eight million copies in twenty-six languages. He has appeared on numerous national bestseller lists, and his titles have been Main or Featured Selections with every major US book club. His recent titles have been named Best Book of the Year by both *Library Journal* and *Suspense Magazine* and have been awarded top pick and starred reviews from *Publishers Weekly*, *RT Reviews*, *Library Journal*, and *Booklist*. His most recent series, *Miramar Bay*, has been acquired for world-wide condensation by *Readers Digest*. In 2019 his feature film screenplay, *Island of Time*, was acquired by David Lipman (*Shrek*, *Iron Man*) and Starlings Entertainment. In 2021 the Thomas Locke series entitled *Emissary* was acquired by Clarion Pictures UK. Currently Davis serves as Writer-In-Residence at Regent's Park College, Oxford University. He speaks around the world on aspects of creative writing.

Of Indian and British heritage, **JYOTI GUPTARA** is a bestselling author of fiction and nonfiction. He lives with a view of the Alps in Switzerland, where he was counted among the "100 Most Important Swiss" by *Schweizer Illustrierte* magazine. By day, Jyoti helps purpose-driven leaders scale their influence by harnessing the power of stories. The County of Los Angeles awarded him a Scroll of Honor for Special Services in philanthropy, literary achievement, and inspiring other young people. He served as Novelist-in-Residence at the Geneva Centre for Security Policy, a UN partner organization, and lectures globally on real-world applications of story and creativity.

Together he and Thomas Locke form a writing partnership that is international, inter-generational, and interracial—and stronger as a result. Stay in touch with the authors at StoryWorlds.ink.

DOWN & OUT BOOKS

On the following pages are a few
more great titles from the
Down & Out Books publishing family.

For a complete list of books and to
sign up for our newsletter,
go to DownAndOutBooks.com.

Short Cuts
Collected Crime Fiction and Nonfiction in Smaller Doses
J.L. Abramo

Down & Out Books
October 2023
978-1-64396-338-9

Twenty years after the appearance of his first short story, *One Hit Wonder* (featuring his private investigator series protagonist Jake Diamond), Shamus Award-winner J.L. Abramo has assembled a collection of previous short crime fiction along with never before published short stories and writings *about* writing in a new anthology.

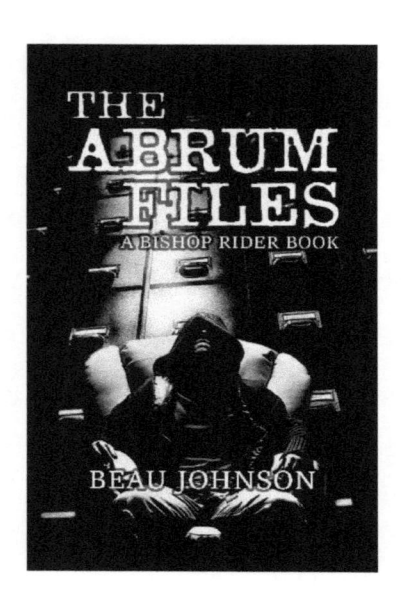

The Abrum Files
A Bishop Rider Book
Beau Johnson

Down & Out Books
October 2023
978-1-64396-339-6

After his sister and mother are murdered by human traffickers, Bishop Rider, a former medic and police officer, spends the remainder of his life hunting not only the men who took his family from him, but every person like them.

He is joined by many partners throughout his war. But when Jeramiah Abrum, the son of one of the men who murders Rider's mother and sister, seeks out Rider to make amends for what his father set into motion all those years ago, a new level of retribution is born.

Happiness is a Warm Gun
Crime Fiction Inspired by the Songs of the Beatles
Josh Pachter, Editor

Down & Out Books
October 2023
978-1-64396-340-2

Roll up for the Criminal Mystery Tour—step right this way!

Seventeen crime stories inspired by the lyrics of the Beatles by a who's who of British and American crime writers including Martin Edwards, Paul Charles, Vaseem Khan, Christine Poulson, Marilyn Todd, Kate Ellis, Tom Mead, John Copenhaver, Michael Bracken, John Floyd, David Dean, Joseph S. Walker, Robert Lopresti, and editor Josh Pachter.

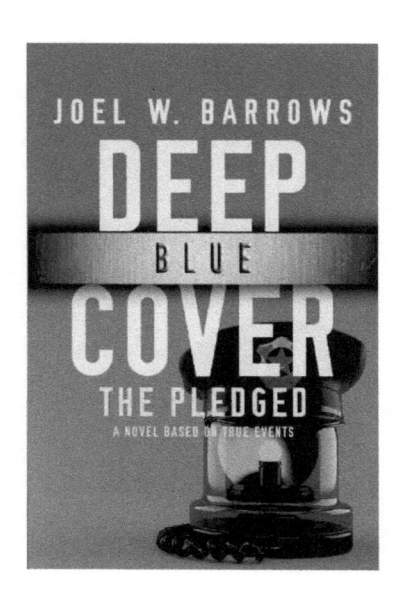

Deep Blue Cover: The Pledged
The Deep Cover Series
Joel W. Barrows

Down & Out Books
October 2023
978-1-64396-341-9

Deputy Jackson Garrett is killed in a hit and run during a routine traffic stop. His death haunts Sheriff Eli Coe. But the investigation hits a dead end. At the same time, rumors swirl that radical elements have infiltrated the sheriff's office. Secrecy shrouds their numbers and intent. Not sure that even his own internal affairs detectives are untainted, Coe brings in an outside investigator.

ATF Special Agent David Ward goes undercover. What he discovers will expose a cancer that lurks in American law enforcement and a plot that threatens democracy.

Milton Keynes UK
Ingram Content Group UK Ltd.
UKHW040642220124
436313UK00015B/113

9 781643 963426